The Unbelievable Misadventures of Olive Finch

By Emmie J. Holland

For Olivia

Because you are the main character in every way possible.

Also, for my family, because this book is filled with the stories of us.

Trigger Warnings

5

Dear reader,

It is my desire to ensure that everyone who picks up this book feels comfortable in doing so. Because of this, I have provided a list of trigger warnings.

Since the trigger warnings include spoilers for this book, you can find the list at the back of the book after the acknowledgments.

ONE

I once heard that in moments of extreme pain, your nerves become completely overwhelmed by the sensory information they receive. You stop feeling anything. That could be totally wrong. In fact, it could have just been some random Facebook meme my grandmother shared, but I'm finding there is some truth to it—at least when it comes to embarrassment. Like, maybe you can be so embarrassed, you stop feeling it.

I can't even feel it.

Actually, that was the problem.

Urgent care is for people with the flu, or strep—maybe even people with strange rashes they need steroid cream for. It is *not* for this monstrosity of an event.

"Olive Finch?" I sit up, looking at the near-empty room. The beige walls and sterile scent seem to mock me as the doctor peeks through the cracked door. I nearly groan at the sight of him. He's young—really young. He's also very much male.

"Yes?" My hands rest on the examination table, my shoulders raised nervously. Any other time, I probably would have been fighting the urge to keep from throwing up, but like I said, I am way past embarrassment at this point.

Another man walks in behind the doctor. He's older, with peppered hair and wrinkles creasing his brow as if he spent most of his life scowling.

At my confused expression, the younger of the two chuckles softly. *Oh shit, why is he actually cute? This literally couldn't get worse.*

"I'm actually in my residency program. Is it alright if I help you today?" he asks. He flashes a smile, straight white teeth, and kind brown eyes. *Ugh.*

"Uh, yeah." I look away briefly. "Sure."

He swings the rolling chair around, sitting backward and propping his forearms on the chair's back. The rolled sleeves of his checkered button-up exposed tone forearms. My eyes scanned the perfectly placed dark hair on his head. *Yikes.*

The scowling *real* doctor is standing stoic in the corner. He doesn't look like he enjoys being here much. I fight the urge to chuckle. Wait until he finds out why I'm here.

"I'm Dr. Jameson. What seems to be the problem?" the young one asks, as if I hadn't already explained the situation to the woman at the desk. Did this guy read the chart? Do I even have a chart at this point?

I laugh, but the sound is too airy and tight to be genuine. "Well," I start, "I decided—" *Oh god, how do I even phrase this? Out with it, Olive.* "I can't get my menstrual cup out."

Someone just put me down. Like a thirteen-year-old chihuahua named Biscuits on his last leg, just let it all end here.

He fights the shock that I *know* was about to cross his face, smiling broadly to hide the fact that he probably wants to laugh. He definitely wants to laugh. Dr. Jameson doesn't, though. He just continues to smile like nothing is wrong before asking questions.

"I'm assuming your menstrual cup is in your vaginal canal. How long has it been in there?"

I clear my throat. "Um, like thirteen hours now."

"And are you currently on your cycle?" he asks.

"Yes." I wince. Not only is this strange man about to dig a menstrual cup out of my vagina, making him the Neil Armstrong of my sex life, but he's also going to be covered in blood. It'll be like *The Purge.*

That's one small step for man, and one giant mess for Dr. Jameson.

"Alright, well, we are going to step out while you get undressed from the waist down." He stands up, opening an overhead cabinet. He grabs out a thin piece of paper all folded up. "You can use this modesty drape, and then we will come in and get it all figured out. Was there anything else you wanted to discuss today?"

My cheeks are on fire. Maybe I was wrong about the embarrassment thing. That statement was *definitely* some random Facebook meme my grandmother posted. Turns out I am capable of feeling embarrassed about this, not that I'm going to admit that to my family.

"No," I almost whisper, fidgeting with my nose ring. "It's just the menstrual cup." I can't handle this. My palms are sweating, and I can almost feel how red my face is.

"Alright." Dr. Jameson smiles brightly, his brown eyes trying to assure me that this isn't the single worst moment of my life, and he isn't about to be almost elbow deep inside me. The first time I'm getting fingered, and it's for *this*.

He moves to the door, Dr. Scowls-a-lot trailing behind him. "We will be back in a few minutes."

The doctor walks out the door and I slouch before standing to grab my phone from the yellow backpack on the floor. I tuck a strand of shoulder-length coffee-colored hair behind my ear. I really need to do something with my hair—maybe dye it.

No. This is just a stress response.

Holding my phone, I click on my family's group chat. I had already called my mom before coming here, but I guess it's time to bite the bullet before the rest of my family finds out—or worse—my grandmother posts it on Facebook.

Me: Guess what happened to me today? Lol.

I quickly strip off my pants and underwear, folding them on the chair and hiding my undergarments so the doctor won't see. *As if that actually matters.* It isn't long before I hear the knock on the door. I grab the modesty drape to maintain some sense of dignity and wait for the doctor to get this damn thing out of my body.

TWO

I'm scrolling through my phone when a text pops up on the screen.

Corrine: Cerebellum is playing a concert tonight on Park Avenue. You in?

Me: You're kidding! Yes. Time?

Corrine: Doors open at 7.

At least something is going right. For the last two hours, I have cringed every five minutes at the memory of Dr. Jameson digging a menstrual cup out of me. For starters, I've never had that much action before, but that is beside the point. I had to go to Urgent Care to get a menstrual cup removed because I couldn't get it out myself.

What kind of twenty-two-year-old *does* that?

I get up off the couch in my small apartment and walk to the small kitchen. The apartment isn't much, but it works for my last year of college, and the best part is I get to live alone. Well, mostly alone. I *do* have a cat named Jafar. He's kind of an asshole, but my therapist said an emotional support animal would help with the whole depression thing.

Jafar weaves between my legs as I gulp down the mediocre tap water that tastes a little of rust. Looking at the clock, I see that it's already five-thirty, so I will need to hustle if I'm going to make it to the concert with Corrine. Park Avenue isn't far from my apartment—only about fifteen minutes. Cerebellum is a band I've been following since their conception, and I would never miss an opportunity to see them.

It sounds absolutely stupid and girlish, but I've been obsessed with Jesse, the drummer, for as long as I can remember. I hope he doesn't mind that some random doctor basically had his entire hand inside me. I cringe inwardly before scratching Jafar behind the ears. He purrs and arches his back.

"You're literally the cutest thing, you little monster," I say in my I-am-talking-to-the-cutest-cat-on-the-planet voice.

Jafar rolls over, exposing the gray and tan tiger-striped fur on his belly. I reach hesitantly to pet him, and he latches his claws into my hand.

"Ouch! You actual asshole!" Prying Jafar from my scratched skin, I go into the bedroom to figure out what I will be wearing. This, of course, could be the night Jesse decides that I'm his twin flame and sweeps me off my feet, literally, and carries me on stage where he announces his undying love for me. *That will never happen, Olive.*

Yeah. I need the perfect outfit.

After digging around in my closet, I go to the giant pile of mostly clean clothes stacked on the wooden chair by my desk. I pick out an all-black jumpsuit. Honestly, it looks like some kind of utility suit, but it's definitely cute.

I leave the top unbuttoned to show the lacy black bralette I chose beneath it. Finally, I grab a simple gold necklace and put on my makeup.

My boots click on the tile floor of the kitchen when I grab my keys and wallet, scratching Jafar on the head one more time for good measure.

"Be good. Don't die."

I lock my door and head out to meet Corinne.

~

"Earth to Olive." Corrine waves her hand in my face. "What are you even doing?"

"Exploring my options." I hold up my phone, revealing the current man's dating profile plastered on my screen. It's an absolute atrocity. Corrine wrinkles her nose at the sight of *Dylan,* 26. Most of his pictures include a dead deer and a mustache with a middle part that puts mine to shame.

"Gross," Corrine comments, running a hand through her chestnut-colored hair. "If you swipe right, I'm sending you thoughts and prayers."

"Ha. Ha. Very funny." I swipe left as we stand on the sidewalk waiting in line to enter the bar. The streetlights are flickering on, and I can almost feel everyone buzzing with excitement.

Winner!

I stare down at my screen. Gabrial, 24. He's cute in a nerdy kind of way. I hold up my phone to show Corrine. "What do we think of Gabriel?" I waggle my eyebrows. "He's in engineering."

Corrine snatches my phone out of my hand, smiling broadly at the screen. "Engineering? Consider your major obsolete. This guy probably has cash." She flips through the photos on his dating profile. "Oh, for sure, this one."

Before I can get my phone back, Corrine has already swiped right on Gabriel. I put the device back in my pocket before she can do any more damage. "Great," I mutter. "I hadn't actually decided yet."

"You're being dramatic."

The line moves, and eventually, we are being ushered into the venue. The lights highlight Corrine's tawny skin, as she practically glows with excitement. We cut a straight line to the bar as the openers set up on stage.

"What can I get for you?" the bartender asks. Her red hair is slicked back in a tight bun, blue eyes striking in the dim lights.

"Just a hard seltzer," I answer, and she hands me my drink, as the opening act begins playing around on stage to check the sound. Soon after, music fills the room.

Corrine and I are finding our places closer to the front, dancing and laughing about anything and everything.

I'm thankful for times like this—the times where nothing matters but music and good vibes.

Cerebellum walks on stage, and I shout along with the crowd, already feeling dizzy after three drinks. I'm now nursing my fourth. I hear the familiar guitar strumming of an older song of theirs called *North*.

I'm instantly lost in the music and the bass. The lights are hot on my skin, and I jump with the crowd, screaming every word to the song. When the first chord of the song *Daffodil* echoes through the venue, the entire crowd erupts again with screams.

Jesse is at the back of the stage, seated at his drum set and playing the instrument with precision. The ink on his arms twists like shadows over his skin in the stage lights. My heart nearly skips a beat when his eyes meet mine and he smiles.

"That's it," I scream over the music. "I'm marrying Jesse."

Corrine tips her head back and laughs, her drink firmly held in her hand as she jumps to the music. "You and at least fifty other girls, Olive."

"Just you watch!" I declare, slurring my words. Corrine and I are definitely drunk and having the time of our lives as the music continues to float through the concert space. I can't remember a time I've ever felt so free.

When the concert ends, we are tripping over each other and laughing, lingering by the stage.

Jesse jumps down from the stage, his forearms flexing as he holds tight to the paper in his hands. My eyes trail over the black t-shirt and jeans he's wearing, desperately wishing to be closer to him.

Corrine whacks me on the shoulder. "Dude, he's looking right at you! What the hell!"

Jesse is standing in front of me and running a hand through his long brown hair before I can gather my thoughts. I giggle obnoxiously, but I can hardly control myself.

"Hey," he says brightly, flashing a smile that would have any girl bowing and kissing the floor beneath his feet. "I've seen you before." He rubs the back of his neck with his hand. "You've been to a lot of our shows. I thought you might want this."

He hands me the paper and I stare up at him with wide brown eyes. The room is practically spinning.

"Thank you," Corrine interrupts, jarring me from my thoughts. She snatches the paper from his hand and shoves it into my chest. It crinkles and I pull it away, looking at the black ink written on parchment. *The setlist.*

Oh. My. God.

"Thank you!" I say, but it comes out too loud. I hiccup and then laugh; Corrine cackling next to me.

"Sure thing," he says before winking and striding away.

My jaw is nearly on the floor when I turn to Corrine. "Did that actually just happen?"

A wide smile breaks across Corrine's face. "Maybe you were right after all. You're definitely marrying Jesse."

I take one look back at the stage before Corrine is ushering me into the parking lot to get into our car.

On the way back to my apartment, I practically demand the driver open the sunroof of the vehicle. I'm halfway out of the car, and before my drunk mind can think better of it, I'm screaming at the top of my lungs to the city beyond.

"I'm going to marry Jesse freaking Schuster!"

I can hear Corrine laughing loudly inside the car.

THREE

The next morning, I wake up with a throbbing headache. Rubbing my temples, I roll out of bed.

That's when the smell hits me.

Cat piss.

"Jafar! You didn't!" I look at my satanic cat all curled up in the corner of my bed as if he didn't just pee everywhere while I was sleeping. Just a few feet away is the giant spot on my floral comforter. The dark spot mocks me.

With my ridiculous hangover, I was hoping to continue my morning by stumbling into the kitchen—cup of ambition and all that.

"I am so close to returning you to the shelter," I seethe.

Jafar meows and hops off the bed, leaving me to rip the comforter from the mattress and slip on a pair of sneakers to run down to the washing machines in my apartment building.

My hair is a mess, and the light streaming through the hall windows is assaulting my brain, making the pounding in my head worse.

When I finally manage to make it back upstairs to the apartment with my comforter promptly washing, I brew myself a cup of delicious coffee. Jafar is basking in the sunlight by my living room window, and he looks so cute I nearly forget why I was mad at him.

I chuckle, taking a long sip before plopping down on the couch to turn on the television. I don't bother changing the channel. I just pull out my phone to see if I've missed any messages.

Corrine: Have you picked your wedding dress yet?

I laugh, glancing at the coffee table where the crinkled setlist is staring at me.

Me: I can't believe he gave me the SETLIST!

I watch some poorly written teen drama about a group of high school kids unearthing small-town secrets. There's murder and a family that gives mafia vibes, which is strange considering—and I cannot stress this enough—they live in an incredibly small town.

My phone vibrates again, and I check the screen.

Corrine: Oh Shit . . .

Attached to the text message is an article about the local band, Cerebellum, and the drum player's new girlfriend. Apparently, *Fefe* was out supporting her new man at the concert last night. My heart sinks.

Me: Fefe? Is she some young grandmother that can't accept she's getting old?

My heart stings in my chest. It was stupid. I know it was stupid, but at twenty-two, the whole *never having a serious boyfriend thing* is getting kind of old.

Corrine: I think her full name is Phoebe. Weird that we didn't even see her there.

Me: We were pretty drunk. Are you going back to Chicago today?

My phone buzzes, and I answer the FaceTime call from my mom. We talk every morning while drinking our coffee. I'm pretty close with her, but right now, I just want to crawl in a hole. I have no prospects, and not a lot of money. I'm not ready to be the town spinster.

"Hey, mom." I take another sip of my steaming coffee.

"You're not going to believe what your grandmother did," my mom starts. She's holding a cup of her own coffee as well and sitting in the living room of what used to be my house in Indiana. Sometimes I miss it, but I plan on staying in Minneapolis after graduation.

"What did she do?"

"She was ordering fudge from that place in Michigan that she likes so much. Not bothering to refresh the page, or actually check what she was doing, your grandmother kept clicking on the two-pound order trying to get it to go through. She ordered two hundred fifty *pounds*." My mom shook her head through the screen. "Thank goodness the fudge shop called and asked if she really meant to order that much!"

I try not to laugh as I lean my phone against the wooden tray at the center of my coffee table and sit back on my couch, running my finger across the soft yellow fabric. I really miss my grandparents, especially my grandfather who has been fairly sick recently. There haven't been many updates on him, though. "Did they charge Grammie for all the fudge?"

"They did. We have to get it worked out with the bank today." My mom sounds exasperated, but these are the types of things that happen that my entire family laughs about later.

"At least she didn't post more family medical information on Facebook. Remember when she posted about Harold's toe?" I finally laugh then. Harold is my brother, and one of my aunts had told my mother and grandmother that he ran over his toe with a car. She told my mom they were going to have to amputate. She was a mess, and my grandmother had posted about the whole ordeal on Facebook. Too bad none of it was real.

"That wasn't funny," my mom scolds while fighting a smile.

"Mom," I start, "It was funny."

A notification pops up on my phone and I pick it up while my mother continues talking about all the Indiana shenanigans. It's mostly updates about my cousin's three-year-old son, Elias. I treat Elias like my nephew. He basically is, and he's absolutely adorable. My cousin got married young since she and her husband had been together forever.

Good for her.

I'm so alone.

I open the notification to see a message from Gabriel in the dating app. I struggle to remember who the guy is, but then it registers. Corrine swiped on him last night at the concert.

Gabriel: Hey!

I quickly type back a response while my mother continues talking.

Me: Hey, what's up?

Gabriel: I saw we matched, and you live close to campus. You go to Junesberg University, right?

Me: Yeah, I'm studying Clinical Psychology.

Gabriel: Sweet! Are you up for a date in the park this afternoon? I have a hammock.

"Mom." I cut her off as I sit up on the couch staring at my phone. "I have to go. I'm making some plans."

She halts. "Oh, is this a date?" she asks as she smiles over her cup. "Who is it?"

"A guy named Gabriel. He's an engineer. He wants to go to the park this afternoon. I guess he lives near campus." My heart is racing with excitement. I'm begging all the gods, the universe, any celebrity that will listen to please, please, *please* not let this man ghost me.

"Okay, Liv. Have fun."

I quickly hang up my FaceTime call with my mother and start planning out the details. We get a time and a place, and I can't stop smiling at my phone.

Hopefully, this one actually shows up.

FOUR

I used to think that I would end up the rich single aunt, toting Jafar around the world and living a life filled with adventure. It turns out, I actually want to fall in love. Don't get me wrong. I see so much value in the single life, but at twenty-two, I feel like I should be kissed at least once.

My palms are sweating, and my heart is pounding in my chest as I walk along the busy sidewalk to Regency Red, the coffee shop near campus where I frequently get the largest iced chai imaginable. I don't think the caffeine will help with my nerves, but at this point, it doesn't even matter. The number of times I've been ghosted by some man on a damn dating app confirms that this will probably be a solo trip to the park and nothing more.

I walk into the narrow entrance of the shop. The blender sounds behind the counter where Ezra is making a smoothie for the person ahead of me. His clear-rimmed glasses are slowly falling down his slightly crooked nose and he pushes them up, glancing toward the door.

I smile and he quickly wipes his hand on a towel, bounding for the counter and switching positions with the other guy working. This is how it usually happens. Ezra is nice enough, and I enjoy our interactions, but he has to be in his thirties. For me, that's a little too old.

"Iced chai?" He asks with a wide smile on his face. "You look nice today."

I glance down at my stonewash, vintage jeans, and mustard yellow crop top. The tan laces on one of my brown boots are coming undone, but I ignore it.

"Uh." I force a tight smile on my face. "Thanks." I touch the sunglasses atop my head. "And yes, to the chai."

"You got it." Ezra hollers to the bald and burly guy who is handing the smoothie to the girl before me. He leans on the counter casually. "Got a hot date?"

A genuine smile slips through. "Yes, actually." I dig into the small black purse slung over my shoulder for my card. "We are going to the park a few blocks from here. I guess he has a hammock."

"How did you meet this mystery man?" he asks, his face falling slightly. Poor Ezra. I wish he were younger. I hear the bells on the door jiggle behind me and fight the urge to look back.

"A dating app," I say. My voice is nearly a whisper. It's not that I'm embarrassed I haven't met someone organically, but the dating app thing still sounds pretty pitiful.

Ezra scowls from beneath his glasses. "Well, I hope he doesn't murder you."

My face twists in an expression that is part confusion and part humor as I slide my card across the counter. Ezra taps his hand over the card once before sliding it back and pushing off the counter to stand up straight.

"It's on me today. Start your date off right."

We stare at each other for a moment, and I wish I could say it's this amazing sexually tense experience where I realize I'm going to fall in love with Regulation Red guy, but unfortunately, it's just awkward.

I laugh a little before glancing at the man in line behind me. He is broad-shouldered and somewhat irritated.

"Olive!" a voice calls from the pickup counter.

"Thanks, Ezra," I say, forcing a brightness to my tone before grabbing my chai off the counter.

As I exit the coffee shop, Ezra calls from the register, "If he turns out to be creepy, just call the store's phone!"

I wave, striding out into the September sunshine baking the asphalt. It's warmer today than I expected.

The perfect day for the park.

~

I'm sitting on the park bench nursing my chai when a text comes through. I pick up my phone quickly, wondering if it's Gabriel.

It isn't.

Tiffany: Did the engineering guy show up?

Me: Not yet. Regulation Red guy was feeling extra flirty today. I got a free drink out of it.

Tiffany: Maybe you should give him a chance.

Me: No

I add a heart emoji to the end of my last text message for good measure before hitting send. Tiffany and I met my freshman year when my absolute monster of a roommate introduced us. We didn't talk much until the winter formal, but we didn't really hit it off until our religion class during the fall semester of my sophomore year.

"Olive?"

I look up to see a tall figure standing over me. He has brown hair, pale skin, and a deep voice. I stand abruptly, holding out my hand for a handshake.

"Hey," I say, wincing as he awkwardly stares at my hand before taking it and shaking it once. I wipe my palm on my jeans, and he lets out a small, nerdy laugh. It instantly makes me feel more comfortable.

"I didn't think you'd show up," he admits. "Sorry, I was running late."

"Oh, it's okay. I was just drinking my chai." I let out a breathy laugh and stiffly gesture to the table where my drink sits dripping with condensation. *Get it together, Olive. You're acting weird.*

He holds a small bag with the fabric of a hammock hanging out the top of the zipper. "I hope you don't mind. I only brought one."

Sweet Jesus. Shit. Damn.

My heart rate speeds up and I laugh again, but the sound is too tight to be genuine. "That's fine," I say.

Gabriel sets up the hammock between two trees in the park and climbs in, patting the spot beside him.

"I never asked," I start. "You are Gabriel, right?"

He laughs again, and it's probably the cutest sound I've ever heard.

"Yeah, I'm not trying to trick you."

Right. I nod and sit sideways in the hammock beside him. My face feels like it's on fire when the fabric forces us even closer together. His entire thigh is touching mine, and I literally cannot believe this is happening right now.

"So, you're an engineer?"

I don't miss the way Gabriel winces at the statement. My stomach drops. *Oh no, did he lie about it?*

"Actually, I'm unemployed. I just graduated last spring." He shifts uncomfortably, and my face heats again at the contact.

"You're twenty-four?" I ask, wondering if maybe he lied about his age.

He runs a hand through his now mussed hair. "It took me a little longer to graduate."

I smile, trying to be encouraging. I can tell he's embarrassed about it, but I don't think he's lying to me. In fact, I kind of like him. "That's fine. I'm set to graduate this Spring."

"Clinical Psychology, right?"

"Yeah!"

The breeze flows through the trees, gently rocking the hammock as a family arrives at the park, fishing a frisbee out of a bag and beginning a game of toss in front of us.

I look over at Gabriel as he watches the child that can't be more than ten tossing a frisbee to his dad. Everything seems right in the world.

Gabriel looks at me and gives a crooked grin. "Can I—" He clears his throat, looking away briefly before his warm gaze returns to mine. "Could I kiss you?"

He must see the shock on my face.

"Not now, I mean." He's quickly trying to backtrack, and my cheeks are on fire. "Like later. Maybe at a later date. Later today." He huffs a laugh. "I'm not very good at this."

"It's okay. I'm not either." I smile up at him. "That would be fine." He glances toward my lips before I hear a loud voice boom across the park.

"Incoming!"

Gabriel's hand snaps out as he catches the frisbee inches from my face. I screamed, I know I did, and I can't help but feel embarrassed at the way I immediately curled up in a ball at the approach of a *frisbee*.

"Thanks, man." The dad wearing cargo shorts, a pale blue t-shirt, and a backward hat catches the frisbee when Gabriel throws it back to him.

"No problem!" he hollers.

We sit in silence for a while, basking in the sun. I check my phone, ignoring the message from Tiffany and seeing that Corrine was already on her way back to Chicago. It's already four forty-five.

"Hey," Gabriel starts. "Do you want to grab some dinner?"

I smile again. I *really* like him. "Sure. That would be great."

~

We decided on Pho, and we've been laughing about anything and everything since we got here. I told him about my grandmother buying two-hundred-fifty pounds of fudge and it sent Gabriel almost rolling on the floor.

Picking up my chopsticks, I grab a piece of tofu from my soup and shove it into my mouth. That's when I see him.

Broth spews back into my bowl, which is totally gross as I attempt to hide my lips behind my hand.

At the front entrance to the restaurant, a familiar face is pulling out a credit card to pay for takeout. I would remember that doctor— correction student doctor—anywhere.

I quickly duck under the table to hide, pretending to pick up a napkin as I swallow the remaining tofu in my mouth.

Gabriel ducks under the table to look at me. "Uh, is everything okay down here?" he asks. "Did I say something wrong?"

"No." I laugh and move to sit up, praying that Dr. Jameson has exited the building.

He hasn't.

When I hit my head on the table trying to sit back up, I notice his eyes are on me from the door, and I want to shrink down into nothing. I want the entire floor to swallow me up and consume me, to save me from this literal *torture*.

Gabriel looks back to the door before turning to face me again. "Who's that?" he asks.

"Oh, no one." I look away, wrinkling my nose. *Just the man that had his whole fist in my vagina yesterday.*

"The *what?*" Gabriel's eyes are wide with shock.

"I said that aloud, didn't I?" *This cannot get any worse.*

Gabriel clears his throat, and I can see the pain on his face. "Maybe this date was a bad idea."

"No!" I snap. "He's a doctor. It was—" I can't, for the life of me, figure out how to tell this story without being completely mortified. "I had an issue yesterday. I'm sorry I'm being weird." Now, I can't stop talking. "It was just really awkward, and I didn't expect to see him here is all. It was a really strange thing, but I swear I'm thrilled to be here on this date." *Olive. Shut up.* "With *you*," I add.

Gabriel chuckles, but it sounds forced. "Okay," he says. "Are you done with your food?"

Oh no.

"Maybe I could walk you back to your apartment." He rubs the back of his neck nervously. "If you want, that is."

I glance back at Dr. Jameson, and he waves before exiting the restaurant. I think Gabriel can see the humiliation on my face. Maybe he feels bad for me.

"I was also thinking we could plan a second date."

My eyes snap to his. My mood is instantly brighter. "That would be great!" I say, but it comes out almost too excited. "I mean, I'd like that."

He smiles then, and this time it doesn't feel forced. "Good."

FIVE

"But did he *kiss* you?" Tiffany asks on the phone the following morning. It's eight-thirty, and Jafar is whining for breakfast.

"No," I answer, recalling the night before. "He just hugged me, but we are supposed to go on a date this Saturday. I don't know if he's planned it yet."

I gather my notebook and place it in my backpack before making my way to the cat food on the stove. Unclasping the top, I put food in for Jafar. He impatiently rubs against my legs, nearly making me trip and fall before I'm able to put his bowl on the ground.

"Aren't we supposed to go to the Curly Fries concert on Saturday?" Tiffany asks. "Wait!" I can hear the excitement in her voice. "Maybe we could invite him! Then I would get to meet him." She's practically jumping up and down on the other side of the phone. "Olive, text him."

"Okay, okay," I say, holding the phone between my ear and shoulder. I pour some water into Jafar's bowl and swing my backpack over my shoulder. "I'll ask him, but I'm making no promises!"

"That's enough for me!" Tiffany hangs up.

I scratch Jafar behind the ear, and he hisses, clearly preoccupied with the food in front of his face.

"Sorry," I mutter. "I have to go to class. Be good. Don't die."

I grab my keys and open the door to my apartment, exiting out in the hallway.

"Damn cat is probably plotting my murder," I mutter before walking down the stairs and onto the streets beyond.

My class in Art History isn't until nine-fifteen, and I have time to stop at Regulation Red for my early morning chai.

~

"How was the date?" Ezra asks from behind the counter. I can tell he isn't extremely excited about it, and I feel bad for hurting his feelings, but I answer honestly.

"It went really well! We are going out again on Saturday."

He rings up my order, and one corner of his mouth pulls up. "I'm glad you didn't die," he says. "Oat milk is on me today."

Sweet Ezra—still giving me free stuff even though I'm talking about a different man in his presence. I almost feel bad for not giving him a fighting chance.

"Thanks, Ezra. You're the best!" I smile brightly, moving to the pickup counter to wait for my beverage.

Ezra mutters something under his breath, and I'm not even sure I want to know what it is as I take my chai from the other employee over the counter.

I wave at him before exiting the door as the bells hit the glass, indicating my departure.

Art History is interesting. *No.* It's actually not. I'm bored out of my mind as I listen to the professor droll on about various artists and the intentions behind each piece. I practically want to fall asleep.

Gabriel: Still want to go out on Saturday?

I hold my phone under the desk and quickly type out my reply.

Me: Of course! I actually had plans to go to a Curly Fries concert with one of my friends. Are you down for coming with us?

I see the bubble with dots for way longer than makes me comfortable and there's a part of me that's afraid I've messed it up. I hardly make sense of the professor's musings that fill the room. It's like the entire world is moving in slow motion, waiting on this one damn response.

He finally replies.

Gabriel: That sounds great!

That sounds great? It took him way too long to write that message. My anxiety kicks in, and I begin second-guessing everything. I'm even having doubts about the outfit I picked this morning. I try to combat my anxiety with logic, telling myself that it means nothing.

Gabriel: Just give me a time and a place and I will be there!

The second message eases my fears and I type out my response, telling him exactly where the concert will be. I can feel the butterflies stirring in my gut, and I hardly notice that class has ended, and the professor is dismissing us.

I can't wipe the smile from my face as I start the walk back to my apartment.

This could totally be it.

SIX

Tiffany and I stand in line at the concert venue for the Curly Fries show. This band is smaller than Cerebellum, but they were an opener for the bigger band once upon a time.

Concerts are one of my favorite places to be. I still remember my first concert as a kid. The band was so excited to see a young audience member, and I distinctly remember them talking about me on stage. My little heart was fluttering at the acknowledgment in the huge sea of people. I've been in love with music ever since.

"Did he say he was still coming?" Tiffany asks from next to me. I'm scrolling through funny videos on my phone. I didn't bother texting him today. After the embarrassing doctor situation, I didn't want to be annoying.

"I haven't heard from him." I shrug.

Tiffany grabs my phone, a frown taking over her expression. She quickly taps something, and I frantically reach for my device.

"What did you say!" I yell, almost bumping into the couple behind me. I cringe at their blatant displays of affection while finally opening up my messages.

Me: Hey! Are you almost here?

"Okay, it's not so bad," I say. "I was worried you were going to say something stupid."

Tiffany laughs. "You probably thought I was going to tell him you were a virgin that's never even been kissed and then beg him to take you tonight."

"Who's a virgin?" I spin around at the familiar deep voice. Gabriel is standing right there, and I can't get my jaw to close from shock.

I laugh nervously, leaning over as I put my phone in my back pocket. "Nobody," I say. I chose a black ribbed tank and jeans for tonight. I fiddle with the hole in the leg of my pants while my cheeks redden.

"Olive is," Tiffany blurts out. "Is that a problem?" she asks.

We can't be friends anymore. She's a monster.

Gabriel ducks under the divider, his tall figure standing next to me. "It's cool," he says. "You should get to choose what you do with your body."

I'm staring. No, I'm drooling. I can't believe he just said that. A small smile forms on my lips when the line starts moving forward.

Gabriel grabs my hand, and his fingers are warm as they thread between mine. At least I know I didn't ruin everything with my erratic and completely insane behavior at the restaurant.

The night is filled with drinks and good music. Gabriel even puts his arm around me a few times and I catch the sly look Tiffany tosses me from within the crowd. Even though Gabriel admitted to knowing none of the music, he's screaming every word by the end of the concert. I won't lie, he's absolutely terrible, but I am too, so it doesn't really matter.

When the concert ends, we all file out onto the street. I flip through my phone, looking at pictures of Elias that my cousin sent. He's at the zoo, feeding a giraffe named Leroy lettuce and looking extremely adorable.

"Who is that?" Gabriel comments from over my shoulder. He's looking down at the picture displayed on my screen.

"My nephew," I say.

"You have a sister?" he asks.

I chuckle. "No, it's my cousin's son. We are fairly close, though. I've called him my nephew since he was born. She doesn't have any siblings, anyway." I smile up at him, noting the small dimple decorating his left cheek. "I have one brother, Harold."

"Is he younger or older?" Gabriel asks.

"Older," I answer. "Eight years older. He lives with his boyfriend back in my hometown in Indiana."

Gabriel's smile widens, and he puts his arm around my shoulders. I can feel the butterflies stirring in my stomach at the contact.

"Do you guys want to go get some food?" Tiffany asks while tucking a blonde strand of hair behind her ear.

"It's almost midnight, but I'm starving," I admit. "Do you guys want pizza?"

"That sounds good!" Gabriel admits, and before I know it, I'm falling.

Hard.

~

It's late—*really* late as Gabriel and I stand in front of the door to my apartment. I can hear Jafar meowing in protest on the other side of the door. He should be okay since I fed him before we left, but that malevolent creature is probably thinking about scratching my eyes out for neglecting second dinner.

"You have a cat?" Gabriel is standing close, and this is the part that always feels so awkward. *Should I tell him I've never kissed anyone before?*

"Yeah, Jafar." I can hardly hold eye contact. "He's kind of a dick."

"Wow," Gabriel laughs. "Insulting your own pet when he can hear you." He raises his brows. "No wonder he's so mean to you."

"I suppose I should be nicer to him."

There's an awkward silence, and I notice Gabriel glancing down at my lips. My stomach is practically in my throat. He had asked me on our first date if he could kiss me, so I knew it was probably coming, but I don't know what to do. Where do I put my hands? What if I am terrible?

"I've never kissed anyone," I blurt out. That ever-familiar feeling of embarrassment rushes through me at the words. It seems that I've been in this place a lot recently, and I wish my grandmother's Facebook meme were true. I wish I couldn't feel this level of shame.

Gabriel reels back a bit. "You—" he pauses, letting out a breathy chuckle. "You don't want to?" he asks.

"No, it's not that." I gesture to literally nothing. What makes it more awkward is Gabriel looks like I was referring to some invisible object right next to us. "I just figured you should know," I finally say.

"Oh." He's smiling again and leaning forward. *Gods above.* "That's not a problem."

Before I know it, his lips are on mine. They're warm and gentle, and I can hardly breathe when he pulls away. It was like a thousand bombs going off in my chest. I try not to smile too hard before fumbling with the keys.

"Well," I begin. "Thank you for the date." I get the key in the keyhole and jiggle the handle. "And the kiss," I add.

"Of course. I'll text you. We should go out again."

"I'd like that." He leans in as I close the door, pressing one more kiss to my lips before saying goodbye and walking away.

When I get into my apartment, I squeal. I can hardly believe it happened. Maybe I won't be a thirty-year-old spinster after all. Too bad for Elias, though. I bet his little three-year-old self really wanted me to be the cool, single, and rich aunt for the rest of my natural life.

"Jafar!" I say while throwing myself on my couch. "I think I'm in love."

SEVEN

It's been two weeks, and I've heard nothing from Gabriel. I've texted him a few times, and he didn't even read them. Well, he could have had his read receipts off. Or maybe he blocked me.

Was the kiss really that horrid?

I sigh as I snack on hummus and carrots from my couch. Jafar is meowing loudly, probably begging for a third breakfast, as usual.

"Shut up, Jafar."

My cat hops up on the couch and wedges himself between me and the container of hummus, rubbing his face on my chin. I think he knows I'm sad.

I set my food down and give up denying the cat his breakfast to go to the pantry and fill his bowl with a few treats. If I can stress eat, Jafar can stress eat too.

I set the bowl on the ground, and he meows in appreciation as I pick up my phone for the five millionth time today.

Still nothing.

I log back onto the dating app and sit back down. It's been long enough. I firmly believe that Gabriel had a miserable time and is trying to avoid me.

I am swiping left on tons of guys holding fish in their profile pictures when a name and photo finally catch my attention. I sit up abruptly, scaring Jafar and making him scurry away to the bedroom.

"Sorry, Jafar," I yell, barely containing the laugh that bursts from my lips. The guy is cute enough, but it's the name that is really getting to me.

Maverick.

"Who name's their kid Maverick?" I ask my cat. He, of course, does not answer my question.

I quickly look through his profile information. He seems nice enough. Kind blue eyes and no fish pictures.

I swipe right.

It's Sunday, so I don't have any classes, but I promised Tiffany that I would meet her at Regulation Red for a coffee. With Corrine out of town, we are a little bit sad. Well, with Corrine out of town, and Gabriel's decision to cosplay as Casper and completely ghost, I'm extremely sad. I need the coffee date.

After dressing myself in distressed jeans and a white t-shirt, I grab a bag and check my hair in the mirror. I've pinned half of it up and put makeup on my face so I can look half decent. Who knows, maybe I will finally run into the *one*.

"Be good. Don't get murdered," I mutter to Jafar before walking out of my apartment.

I take the stairs, as usual, to avoid any awkward elevator conversations. While I'm halfway down the steps, I start questioning my decision entirely. What if I'm missing out on the opportunity to meet someone because I'm being anti-social, and I keep taking the stairwell?

I bound up the two flights of stairs and re-enter the hallway near my apartment. I opt for the elevator instead, hoping that some handsome and somewhat nerdy man will enter the small space and waltz into my life.

No luck.

The walk to the coffee shop is equally boring. I shoot a few text messages to my mom, updating her about my day. Then I text Corrine and ask for the latest information from Chicago. She responds promptly, and I'm glad to hear that she's gotten to spend time with her nephew Diego. It makes me miss Elias even more.

When the door opens to Regulation Red, I scan the few tables for Tiffany. She isn't here yet, so I promptly stride up to the counter where Ezra is waiting for me. He seems almost more hopeful today than he was yesterday.

Maybe I'm really looking pitiful this morning.

"Good morning, beautiful," he says. I try not to wince at the endearment. He's never been anything but nice, but it still gives me the ick. He's just a little old. Not old enough to make me uncomfortable, but old enough to never be a true option in my life. "Chai today?"

"Yeah, but can I get it hot?"

Ezra raises his brows. "Living on the edge." He takes my card and runs it through the reader. "How's the mystery man? The one you had a date with."

I run my tongue along my teeth. "It didn't really work out," I admit. I expect Ezra to perk up at that, but he actually frowns. He really is a nice guy. Maybe if I knew someone closer to his age, I could set him up. Well, my cousin Josephine is his age, but she is already happily married. She also doesn't live here anyway.

"Sorry about that," he says, and his voice sounds genuine. "Free oat milk today, and a free pastry on me. What would you like?"

I laugh a little and look at the display case for whatever sweet treat my body is craving. I go for a basic coffee cake covered in cinnamon sugar and caramel drizzle.

"Good choice," Ezra says.

Tiffany approaches behind me and nearly startles me when she taps my shoulder.

"You ready for this coffee date?" she asks.

"I guess I have time for coffee since Gabriel totally ghosted me," I joke. It doesn't sound convincing.

"Awe! You should perk up." Tiffany steps up to the counter to order. "I'm a catch." She orders her drink, and I notice that her oat milk is *definitely* not free. It almost makes me feel bad, but I'm too distracted by the soft music and murmurs of the customers.

We find a seat at a small table and start discussing our classes. Tiffany lives off of campus, but I'm thankful that she makes time to drive in on the weekend to hang out with me. It gets lonely with just Jafar. Besides, I'm pretty sure Jafar hates me.

"Is Ezra still giving you free oat milk?" Tiffany asks while taking a sip of her drink across from me.

"Of course," I say. I'm trying hard not to mope, but things seem pretty hopeless right now. "Too bad Gabriel didn't work out. I really thought things were going well."

"Especially after he kissed you!" she adds. "I thought for sure you were on to something. He was also really cute and nice. I got tons of respectful vibes from him." She places her cup on the table. "You know we live to see that."

"Of course."

Tiffany quickly changes the subject, and I'm thankful for that. We spend a good hour talking over anything and everything. She's excited about graduation, and I have to admit that I am too. I was looking into getting a job here after seeing one advertised in the Career Connections offices on campus.

After we leave, I hug Tiffany and make my way to the grocery store to buy something to eat for dinner tonight. I will probably end up making a box of vegan mac and cheese, but it doesn't hurt to come up with something to cook.

I'm looking at the produce when I hear him.

"Olive?" Gabriel is standing right next to me wearing a fitted black t-shirt and jeans. I feel like my eyes are deceiving me, and I can feel the sinking feeling settle in my gut.

"Oh," I say. There's a long pause. *Real smooth, Olive.* "Hi, Gabriel," I finally add.

He's holding a bag of apples and his eyes are flicking wildly around the room. Maybe he was secretly married or something.

"I just wanted to say I'm sorry," he blurts out.

I try to shrug it off. It's been two weeks. He's only apologizing because he ghosted me. I feel anger bubble up in my chest like a simmering stew waiting to erupt over the edges of a pot. I have to keep my composure.

"It's fine," I answer, casually tearing a plastic bag away and looking at the radishes in front of me. I don't even like radishes. "It's been two weeks. You didn't enjoy the date. No harm done." I can't help the bitterness seeping into my tone.

"It's not that," he steps closer. When I look up at him, I notice that he's nervous. Frantically running a hand through his hair. "I—uh—" He can hardly get a word out. "It's a little personal."

"Oh," I raise an eyebrow at him—challenging him to continue.

"I was in the hospital."

"Oh," my tone is flat, and my eyebrows instantly lower together and crease.

Oh. My. God. I'm a bitch.

"Yeah," he starts, still nervously fidgeting where he stands. He breathes a laugh. "It was a mental health facility. I was actually having a bit of a hard time before we met."

As if things couldn't get any worse. The guy took a grippy sock vacation. Now, I don't blame him, I've battled with depression too. It's the entire reason I have Jafar. It's just that this situation is completely unbelievable. I can't even tell if he's telling the truth, but he seems genuine, so I try to give him the benefit of the doubt.

"I'm really sorry to hear that, Gabriel." My tone is gentle as I try to ease whatever worries he may have. The last thing I want is him thinking that I'm judging him. "I had a fun time on the date, too." I can't believe I say the next part. "I wish it would have worked out."

"Yeah," he says, his eyes briefly connecting with something behind me. "Me too." He lifts his bag of apples and nods his head in the direction of the check-out. "Well, see you around, Olive."

"See you."

I'm left standing there, dumbfounded and trying to put the ridiculous number of radishes I picked up in my discomfort back on the shelf.

That's when I hear a laugh behind me. To my horror, it's Dr. Jameson.

Someone, please kill me.

"I remember you," he says while selecting lettuce from the produce section. "You came into my office almost a month ago."

I cringe, all of those embarrassing feelings returning with a vengeance. "I did," I answer honestly.

I turn to face him then, remembering the way he was laughing. "Were you eavesdropping on me, Dr. Jameson?"

"You can call me Milo," he says. "And I may have heard a thing or two." He smiles and flashes those ridiculously white teeth again. "I'm sorry your date didn't work out."

My face deadpans. "Tragic, really."

"Well," he starts, a sly look on his face. "Here's my card if you ever want to try a different contestant."

He hands me a card with his face and name on it. There is a phone number and a fax number. I take it and simply stare at the small piece of paper in my hand.

"Are you supposed to ask patients out?" I ask, looking up at him. He's fairly tall and his skin has a subtle tan leftover from the summer. It's impressive considering it is now October in Minneapolis. Maybe he's one of those doctors that goes tanning and gets their teeth whitened.

Oh my god, maybe he gets his butthole bleached or his balls waxed or something embarrassing.

I try not to laugh at my own thoughts.

"Well, you're not really a patient anymore," he says before looking me up and down. "Not since we took care of the—" He pauses, and I know exactly what he's thinking. I suddenly want to crawl under a table. "Issue," he finishes.

"Right," I say, shoving the card in my pocket. I promptly decide that I am *never* going to call Dr. Milo Jameson.

Not ever.

"It was good to see you." I turn around and strut to the counter to buy my one bunch of radishes. Unfortunately, I forgot to get anything for dinner.

Vegan macaroni, it is.

EIGHT

"Show Auntie Liv what you got." My cousin's voice sounds out of my phone's speakers and my heart clenches in my chest as I watch Elias prance around their living room.

He walks up to the phone camera, and I can hardly see what is on his shirt because he's too close, then half in the frame, and then gone. "I got a *Spidey* shirt," he announces.

I giggle at how excited he sounds. It's been about a week and a day since the Gabriel incident, and the sorrow is finally subsiding.

Kind of.

"Your mom got him the shirt." Josephine turns the camera and props her phone up while she sits on her tan couch. I can hear some kid's show playing in the background and Elias is now banging some toys together as if they're fighting. "How was your date? Your mom was telling me about it."

I sigh, leaning back on my couch and not bothering to hold my phone up for my entire face to be in the frame. I minimize the FaceTime call because, let's be honest, if Elias isn't in the picture, it doesn't really matter.

"I can't believe she didn't tell you." I scroll through the pictures of the concert we went to. It's hard to admit, but I actually really liked Gabriel. This breakup feels kind of sad. *It's not even a breakup, Olive. Get it together! It was like two dates.* "He ghosted me."

"That seems to be the norm nowadays. What is wrong with people?"

"That's not all." I keep my tone bored as I continue scrolling through my phone. "Turns out he was in a mental health facility for suicidal thoughts."

"You're kidding!" My cousin is staring at the screen again, and I fight back a smile.

"Dead serious."

"You are the main character," she says while laughing. "That doesn't even sound real!"

I get a notification from my dating app just as Elias asks for mac-and-cheese for lunch.

"I have to go," Jo says quickly.

"That's fine." I know I sound super bummed, but I can't help it. The Gabriel thing has me all kinds of emotional.

"Tell Liv bye," Jo says to Elias.

"Bye Elias! Love you!" I try to make my tone sound brighter for my nephew. He deserves it.

"Bye Jafar!"

Jo and I both laugh at that. Elias is already off running and carrying on about being hungry.

"He would," I say finally, a smile actually crossing my face.

"Bye, Liv."

"Bye."

When I hang up the FaceTime call, I quickly scroll over to the dating app on my phone. Turns out I have a new match and a message. I'm less than hopeful, though.

Jafar jumps up on the couch and stretches his sneaky little body up the back end, extending his paws and digging his nails into the fabric. I sit up and swat him away.

"Get off!" I yell.

Jafar hisses at me and tries to bite my thumb. I shake him off. Satan himself must have sent this malevolent ball of fur. Maybe he's the reason I'm having such a horrible time with my love life.

What love life, Olive?

"Oh my god, Maverick?" I literally don't think I've ever met a guy named *Maverick* before. Looking at his photos, I realize he is kind of cute. That sounds like an asshole move, but I am also sad. I decide I don't care and check the message.

Maverick: You up for a movie?

I sigh and type out my response. Honestly, my standards are dropping into the fiery pits of hell at this point. I'd say yes to my cousin's train wreck of a childhood best friend at this point.

Actually, scratch that. Names that start with *j* are an absolute no. I probably wouldn't say yes to him. I'm not *that* desperate.

Speaking of *j* names, I still have Dr. Jameson's card somewhere in this messy apartment. I should throw that thing away.

Me: I love movies. What were you thinking?

It doesn't take long to get a response from Maverick. I'm scrolling through his pictures and deciding if he looks like he might murder me when the new message pops up.

Maverick: We could go somewhere near you, or we could chill at one of our places?

This is bad news. A guy asking to go to your place on the first date is never a sign of noble intentions. Then again, I'm twenty-two and I literally just had my first kiss like three weeks ago.

My life is so sad.

Me: Sure. You could come here?

I'm safer in my own home, right? He doesn't seem like an ax murderer, and he definitely doesn't look like a crazy rapist. His name also starts with *m* so, that's a good sign.

I'm probably making the biggest mistake of my life.

If I text Tiffany and tell her what's going on, she can come to save me. She would probably throw hands if she really had to. I wince because Tiffany would probably *not* throw hands with an ax murderer. I mean, *I* wouldn't throw hands with an ax murderer.

Making what is probably the worst decision of my life, I message Maverick my address and set up a time for a movie tonight. I chose six o'clock because it isn't so incredibly late that it sounds like a booty call. Can it be a booty call if the man has never seen your booty? What if no man has ever seen your booty?

I huff and pick said booty up off the couch, striding to the coffee machine to make my second cup of the morning since I really can't face Ezra today. He will probably ask about my non-existent dating life and try to give me free things.

"You know, Jafar," I say while plopping back down on the couch in front of my television. "This all really sucks." I stare at my demon of a cat. My brown eyes flick to the scratches on my hands and back to the little monster. "You'd attack a man if he tried to ax murder me in my own home, right, Jafar?"

My cat just stretches his paws up the couch again and begins kneading his way through every last inch of fabric.

"That was a stupid question." I take a sip of my coffee. The liquid is hot, and I quickly set the mug down on the table before I burn my tongue anymore. "It was a really dumb question, Jafar. You'd probably be the one doing the ax murdering."

Jafar rolls over and exposes his belly, using his paws to rub at his ears and face. The move is so cute that I can't resist reaching down and petting him. To my surprise, he actually lets me this time and I realize what my nephew Elias might see in him—the reason I haven't *actually* taken him back to the shelter despite my many threats.

"You're pretty cute, you rascal."

NINE

I've been frantically cleaning my apartment all day like a psychotic person. I texted Tiffany to let her know what was going on, and she promised to stop by within an hour if she didn't hear from me, so I'm hoping it doesn't take an hour to ax murder someone.

Of course, it takes way less than an hour to do that.

It doesn't matter. I'm totally chancing the murder thing, but I'm also chancing the getting-some-action thing. My stomach twists in knots as I pace my apartment. Jafar can clearly see that I'm stressed and promptly removes himself from the situation by going to my bed.

I sincerely hope he doesn't piss on my comforter again.

A knock sounds at the door, and I panic. I can feel every last butterfly that is whizzing around in my belly as I approach the door. I shouldn't be this nervous, but I am. Even so, I'm not expecting much from this particular guy. I hate to say I'm not over Gabriel because we only went on two dates before he ghosted me, but it's the truth and what do I have if I don't have my honesty?

I open the door.

"Olive, right?"

The boy standing in front of my door is actually super cute. He's wearing rounded glasses and a wide smile as I open the door wider. He doesn't smell like bleach or sawdust, so that rules out several ways he could have been plotting to kill me.

"That's me," I say when I notice Jafar making a run for it from the other side of my apartment. I quickly close the door and then internally panic because I just confirmed my identity and then promptly slammed the door in my date's face.

I crack the door a little and shove my leg at the bottom to make sure Jafar doesn't escape.

"Sorry." I try to smile and look like I'm not completely crazy—or completely sad. "I have a cat named Jafar, and he's kind of a runner."

Maverick laughs and it's literally the cutest sound I've ever heard. He's still smiling when I open the door and let him in. As he walks past me, I catch a whiff of one of those mahogany teakwood candles they sell at the store in the mall here. It's not bad, but it's nothing fancy.

Not that I need fancy. I wasn't expecting five-hundred-dollar cologne or anything. Oh man, I'm so nervous.

"Do you like water?" I ask before biting my tongue. "I mean, would you like water?"

"Sure." Maverick has his hands shoved in the pockets of his jeans. He's standing in the middle of my kitchen, so I gesture to the yellow couch and the television.

"Movie's in there. I can make some popcorn, too."

The boy nods and walks over to the couch. I glance sideways at him, expecting him to look stiff and nervous, but find him reaching down to coax Jafar from his new hiding place beneath the coffee table.

"He probably won't bother with you," I mention while tearing open the cardboard box filled with microwavable popcorn before throwing it in and pressing the button designated for popcorn.

"That's alright." Maverick sits back on the couch, one arm splayed across the back of the sofa. I smile while bringing over two glasses of water and setting one on the coffee table while handing him the other.

"What are we watching?" he asks.

That's when a true smile appears on my face. I am so proud of my weed-out tactic I can hardly contain myself.

When the microwave beeps, I prance into the kitchen and pour the buttery snack into a giant mixing bowl.

"Only the best movie known to man." I sit down on the couch next to Maverick and leave a careful distance while reaching forward for the remote. When I press play, it becomes painfully obvious what movie we are watching. "It's *Mamma Mia!*," I supply—just in case he has no idea. Which, if he doesn't, goodbye Maverick.

He doesn't groan or launch into a long speech about how the movie is completely horrid or ridiculous, so that's a good sign.

"Have you seen it before?" I ask.

Maverick chuckles and runs a hand through his carefully placed strands of brown hair. They become just a little mussed, and I can't say that I don't like it.

"I can honestly say that I've never seen it. Will there be singing?"

"Oh, absolutely." I wonder if he can see the happiness on my face. It's the truth—I do feel happiness. After a long week of moping, I could use a date like tonight.

Maverick smiles down at me and promptly puts his arm around my shoulders. At first, I'm completely stiff. My eyes widen slightly before I grow more comfortable and lean into him.

The opening scene brightens the screen, and we are met with calm waters, soft singing, and three names before cutting to a man on a motorcycle.

I wanted to eat popcorn, but I didn't dare. Not with Maverick sitting right next to me, and especially not with the way he keeps glancing sideways at me. It's hard to focus on the movie when I'm hyperaware of every little movement and every place our bodies are touching.

Maverick's arm is still around my shoulders, his thigh pressed firmly to my own, and when he starts moving his thumb gently along my shoulder, every nerve in my body screams at me.

What were you thinking, Olive? A movie in your apartment for a first date. Of course, this guy wants something from you!

When I look over at his hooded gaze, alarm bells start going off in my mind.

The truth is, I feel like an absolute harlot. I can't believe I invited a man I met online over to my apartment to watch a movie. He absolutely didn't want to watch a movie. The worst part of the entire situation is that there is a small part of me that *knew* all of that and still did it anyway.

Maybe Gabriel was okay with my inexperience, but it won't always be that way. I'd love to say the right guy will come along and won't care, but in my sorrowful state, that logic seemed to launch itself out the window. I knew what was going to happen, and I wanted it.

When Maverick leans forward with his lips parted, I close my eyes, and I don't hesitate.

The first brush of his lips is gentle, and I can't say that it's unpleasant. Despite all of my guilt and self-loathing, I actually like it, especially when his fingers twine in my hair, and I stop hearing the movie altogether.

I'm near breathless by the time Maverick pulls away, and he still smells like that candle, but I also catch a whiff of some sort of mint on his breath. I can still taste it too as he trails kisses down my neck.

My breath catches, and I try to be okay, but my mind screams in response.

What does he think he's doing?

I don't stop him though—not as he kisses down to my collarbone or as he tugs at the hem of my shirt to expose cleavage.

"Is this okay?" he asks.

Thank god he is at least getting consent, but I wish I knew, buddy!

"Um."

He hears my hesitation and looks up at me. I can see the hidden disappointment behind his eyes. He absolutely did not come here to watch Sophie attempting to learn who her real father is.

"It's not, is it?" Maverick asks the question as if I've just told him I murdered his pet goldfish.

"No!" I say, a little too loudly. "This is fine. I just—" *Do I tell this man I'm a virgin?* "Maybe just kissing." I nod my head once. "For now."

I can see the corner of Maverick's lip pull up, but there's still something in his eyes that tells me he's disappointed.

Before I know it, his hands are on me, and his mouth is on my breast. I can't say that I didn't like it—I really can't, but what I *can* say is that I have no emotional attachment to the man currently swirling his tongue around my nipple and that in itself causes me to pause. He notices the shift in my mood.

"I'm sorry," I say, shaking my head. "It's just—" I don't know how to explain this to him. "I'm a virgin."

I don't miss the look of panic that crosses his face before Maverick quickly wipes it away. "Oh," he says. "That's—that's fine." He sits up, running a hand through his hair as his eyes flick wildly around the room. I can hear Jafar meow by his food bowl. He probably wants a second dinner.

"It's getting late,' I say as I shift to the edge of the couch. My hands are firmly planted, and I wish I could curl in on myself and disappear. My cheeks heat with embarrassment.

"Right." Maverick gets up and grabs a piece of popcorn before tossing it in the air and catching it in his mouth. "I can go."

"I didn't mean to kick you out!" My eyes are pinned on his. I can tell everything I need to know by his face. This was *never* going to work. "I mean, you can stay and watch the movie if you'd like."

"I have to work in the morning anyway," he supplies.

"Right." I give him a quizzical look. "What is it you do again?"

"Um, I work in graphic design."

"Oh," my voice sounds defeated. "That's cool." I honestly don't know if I should get up and hug him or not. I mean, his mouth was just on my boob. It still feels uncomfortable.

I stand and stretch out my hand. "Well," I say. "It was nice to meet you."

He awkwardly takes my hand and shakes it once. "Nice to meet you too, Olive. I'll see you around?"

"For sure."

As Maverick walks out my door, I realize I will probably never see him around, and if I do, I will run in the other direction.

I release a sigh and hear Jafar taunting me from where he is now perched on the couch.

When I close the door, I turn around to face my cat and scowl at him for mocking me. "Oh, shut up."

It isn't long before my head hits the pillow and the sadness returns.

TEN

I wake up the following morning with a deep well of self-loathing bubbling inside my stomach like molten rock churning in the belly of a volcano just waiting to erupt.

Not that I didn't enjoy everything Maverick did. It all had been—wrong.

If it had been Gabriel, things might have been different. I liked Gabriel. We went on two successful dates where we were getting to know one another. He asked me about my family and not once did I feel pressure around him.

I can't blame Maverick. In fact, he was extremely respectful. He respected the hell out of my boob, especially. It was my fault. I knew what I was doing when I responded to his message. Inviting him over to my apartment for a first date wasn't really a date at all. It was an opportunity to stop feeling sorry for myself and make myself more desirable by gaining experience.

That's where the self-loathing was coming from.

Inviting a guy over to make out with you so you'd be more appealing lowered my standards into the fiery pits of hell. I don't want that to be me.

Staring at my ceiling, I hug my pillow to my chest. I'm thankful that my comforter doesn't smell like cat pee this morning, but I'm not thankful that it's Monday and I have Art History again.

Checking the time on my phone, I sit up and throw my fresh-scented blanket off my legs before climbing out of bed to the pile of clothes on my desk chair. Fall has really descended on Minneapolis, and I decide to embrace the season by wearing black *Doc Martin's*, sheer black tights, a black skirt, and a cream blouse.

After putting on makeup, I don't feel so helpless and I'm just about ready to leave the apartment.

I step on something that sticks to my shoe when I walk into the kitchen where I keep Jafar's food. Peeling it from my boot, I notice that it's a business card with a familiar name plastered everywhere.

Dr. Jameson.

I turn the card over in my hand and my stomach twists. Maybe it wouldn't be so bad if I give him a chance. After last night, I really don't think the dating apps are serving me well. Meeting someone organically *does* sound more appealing.

So organic that the man has felt your literal insides, Olive.

I wince, but I can't bring myself to put the card down. I grab my phone and open a new message, typing in the series of digits that make up Dr. Jameson's number. I can actually feel my knees shaking.

Me: Still considering a date? You did fish a menstrual cup out of my lady cavern. You kind of owe me dinner.

I stare at the message for a solid five minutes before pressing send and immediately closing my eyes. If I shove my phone in my backpack and never look at it again, then what I just did can't be real.

Right.

When I get outside, the air is brisk and swift as it rocks the shades of red and gold in the trees above. I should have considered a jacket, but I don't bother going back up to my apartment to retrieve one. I won't have time if I want to sit for breakfast before class starts.

When I get to Regulation Red, there's actually a line and I'm stuck staring at the menu for a solid ten minutes. I don't dare check my phone. I don't think I could handle a response. I almost never send messages that are so *forward*.

"The largest iced chai with oat milk?" Ezra asks while peering at the screen and typing in my order.

I smile and nod. "I could also go for a bagel this morning."

"Ah, that's going to cost you." Ezra's eyes meet mine briefly and he has a wide smile splayed across his face. "Oat milk is always free for you though, Olive."

"Thanks, Ezra."

After getting my breakfast, I find a spot at one of the small tables in the coffee shop. The seating area is almost like a greenhouse with red-tinted glass that gives the entire place a red glow. It fits the name.

The sound of espresso grinding, and soft murmuring fills the room as I sip on the iced chai I ordered.

It isn't long before a body drops in the chair across from me and I jolt. Ezra isn't wearing his uniform, which I didn't notice before, and he has one of the pastries from the glass display up front.

"I'm not actually working today," he admits. "Care if I join you?"

I really don't need Ezra thinking that we are on a date, but I can't lie and say I don't appreciate the company.

"That's fine," I supply. I offer him a wane smile and reach down into my bag to grab my phone and check the time. I had briefly forgotten about the text message, but when I see a response on my screen, my heart races.

Dr. Jameson: I guess I do owe you dinner. Are you available on Sunday?

"Who is it?"

"Hm?" I look up at Ezra with my phone still tightly gripped in my hand.

He nods to the device. "Who has you smiling? Another date, I suppose."

"It's—" I set my phone upside down on the wooden table. I sigh because I *do* need someone to talk to about this, and maybe if I go on about my dating life, Ezra will realize that he really isn't in it.

Not that your dating life really exists.

"It's a doctor." I blink. "Well, he's in his residency program. I had to go in over a month ago and I ran into him outside of the office. He gave me his number."

"Isn't that against whatever rules they have about doctors and patients?" Ezra takes a bite of what looks like some flakey pastry with raspberry jam.

"I'm not actually his patient." I wince. Maybe it was against the rules. "It was a one-time deal."

"And now you're dating him?" he asks. "You do realize he will be at least twenty-six if he's in a residency program?"

I take another sip of my chai and set the cup down. "I mean, I suppose."

"Does that bother you?" Ezra has one eyebrow raised, and he's staring at me with so much intensity that I feel like a caged animal desperate for escape. *That question was so loaded.*

I can't help the way I glance at the door briefly.

"I mean, does the age bother you? Is twenty-six too old?" Ezra takes a sip of the hot coffee he brought from the bar. "What if he was like, thirty-four?"

I want to ask Ezra if he's thirty-four. It seems about right considering everything. "Thirties might be too old for me." I give Ezra a sympathetic look. "A five-year difference wouldn't be so bad. I don't know."

"Well." Ezra offers a small smile, and I can see that he's truly trying to be there for me. My heart warms at how genuine he is being, and I wish I could find someone better suited for him. "You will never know unless you try."

I feel my phone vibrate against the table and I glance down again. It's face down, so I can't see who texted me, but I already know who it probably is.

Ezra nods toward my phone and encourages me to pick it up.

Dr. Jameson: If I promise not to make fun of you, will you say yes already?

I smile when I read the text. Ezra is right about the age-gap issue, but I will never know unless I try.

Me: How is six-thirty?

Dr. Jameson: I'll be there.

ELEVEN

I'm pacing around my apartment like a tiger in a cage and there's no stopping the nerves that are gliding through my body like they decided to join the ice rink's free skate period.

Maybe Ezra was right, and Dr. Jameson is way too old for me. The only thing that I know is he told me to dress casually, and he let me know he was excited to take me out. Considering the last guy I was with just wanted in my apartment and possibly my pants, I'd say things are running a bit smoother.

The knock on the door has my heart nearly stopping in my chest. Jafar lets out a soft meow, and I'm certain he's mocking me.

"Oh, shut up," I glower.

When I open the door, Dr. Jameson is standing there wearing a black crewneck sweater, brown pants, and sneakers. He looks put together and absolutely perfect as his warm eyes catch my own and my breath catches.

I pull at the hem of my chunky sweater and grab my leather jacket. He said casual, but I wasn't going to show up looking like a hermit.

You are kind of a hermit.

Dr. Jameson rubs the back of his neck in a nervous gesture, and I'm actually thankful. At least I know I'm not the only one freaking out.

"There's a fall festival going on," he begins. "I may have looked through your Instagram and saw that you liked music. They have a few bands playing and some fall-themed games. I thought we could grab a bite from one of the food trucks." He shoves his hands in his pockets and rocks back on his heels. "We don't have to stay out late."

I think he notices the huge smile on my face because I watch as the corner of his mouth pulls up. "That sounds great." I turn around and point to Jafar. "Be good. Don't die."

I don't miss the way Dr. Jameson chuckles as we make our way out of my apartment.

When we get to his car, he opens the door of the *Subaru* on my side and gestures for me to get in. Before I know it, we are on our way to wherever he is taking us. I don't feel fear—just excitement.

"So," I start, breaking the silence. "How is—" I pause, trying to find the right word. "Doctoring?" I supply.

Dr. Jameson laughs a little before flipping on his right turn signal.

We love a man who uses turn signals.

"It's fine. I'm pretty busy with my residency program, but I'm enjoying it."

I fidget with a small hole in my jeans. "I'm glad you're enjoying it." I can't stop the next statement from flying out of my mouth. "Get your hands in a lot of vaginas, I take it?"

He laughs then, flexing his hand on the steering wheel. I notice he's wearing a silver ring on his thumb. The butterflies in my stomach flutter and I look away, watching the road in front of us.

"No, actually," he answers. "Your case was rather rare." He glances sideways at me. "I did promise I wouldn't make fun of you, though, so we can drop it."

"But you want to?" My face flushes as I think of all the ways he could have taken that statement. "Make fun of me, I mean."

He raises a hand to his chest in mock offense. "I'm surprised you would even think that." I can see the smile he's trying to hide.

There's a pause before I think of my next question. "And how is Dr. Scowls-a-lot? I assume he's mentoring you or whatever."

Dr. Jameson allows the smile to break across his face, and I get a glimpse of his straight white teeth. *Damn.*

"Dr. McMillian?" *Okay, so, not scowls-a-lot.* "He's kind of a hard ass, so you have that part correct. I think he's alright, but I can never truly tell." He winks at me, and surprisingly, it doesn't feel cheesy. *At all.* "I'll have one more year of residency after this, and then I'm on my own. It's a little nerve-wracking. Dr. McMillian knows what he's doing, though." His brows furrow as if he's thinking about how to describe the doctor mentoring him. "He's helpful."

I bite the inside of my cheek gently. "Better at fingering women, then?"

"Damn," Dr. Jameson says. "You really want me to make fun of you, don't you?"

"No." Maybe that was too much. It was a pretty crude joke. I *never* make those. What is happening to me? "I just—" I don't know how to finish the sentence. "I'm not sure." I look away, watching the city slowly pass by out the window. The sound of music twists in the air as we approach the parking lot. Dr. Jameson hasn't said anything, and I'm sure I've messed it all up.

He turns left into a small lot with only a few spots available. "He knows a lot about medicine." Dr. Jameson finally breaks the silence. He smiles and I catch his eyes turning toward me to gauge my reaction. "But to answer your question about his talents in comparison to mine, no."

He raises a brow while the car comes to a stop. My cheeks are on fire as I catch his meaning, but before I have a chance to think too hard about it, Dr. Jameson is opening my door.

As we walk, I notice the golden hue that has descended on the city. It's the light that comes just before dusk. There are people laughing and playing games up ahead as I peer beyond the barricade blocking off the street.

Dr. Jameson laces his fingers through mine, and I clear my throat to hide the way my heart sped up at the contact.

"What about you?" he finally asks as we approach the festival. "You know I'm a doctor, but what do you do?" There's a brief pause, and he places his free hand in his pocket. "I know you're twenty-two from your chart, but we can just pretend I don't know that if you'd like. I'd be happy to ask."

I laugh a little at that. Now I just need to figure out if Dr. Jameson is in his thirties. He certainly looks younger.

"I'm in my last year of school and majoring in clinical psychology," I provide.

"That's a good choice. What made you want to do that?"

I consider giving him the easy answer, but the truth is, I want him to know more about me than my age, height, and weight.

And, of course, the feel of your lady parts.

"Originally I was undecided." I fight the small amount of embarrassment that surfaces. People should probably know exactly what they are doing when they go to college, but I only had a vague idea. "I ended up really loving a Queer Studies course and I would have loved to major in that. I didn't think it would pay off my loans, and I didn't want to go the professor route, so I chose clinical psychology after a psych class." I feel like I'm rambling, but Dr. Jameson seems to be listening intently, so I push forward. "I started seeing the intersections of psych and GSWS and realized I could combine the two to work with LGBTQ youth. I could do something I was passionate about, and really help others."

He smiles down at me, and my chest warms at the sight. Dr. Jameson nods and looks pensive as we cross the barrier into the fair lined with booths and games. There are stalls offering colorful clothing, popcorn, and face-painting for children. His grip tightens on my hand momentarily.

"I really like that," he finally says. "I picked Emergency Medicine, but I didn't go the ER route. Most people who go to Urgent Care don't have family doctors or insurance. It was a way to help people who are sick and give them the quality care that a family practitioner would give. Even if they're only in my office for a small amount of time."

"Dr. Jameson—"

"Milo," he corrects with a wide smile.

"*Milo*," I say. "That sounds really noble, but Dr. Scowls-a-lot doesn't seem like the type to be that kind."

He sighs, leaning his shoulder into me jokingly. "Well, you know, we can't all be perfect."

"Of course."

But you probably are.

The fair isn't incredibly crowded, and I spot a booth where they are offering pumpkins and paints. I immediately drag *Milo* to the stand, smiling because I can hear whatever band is playing, and I'm pretty sure this is the best date I've ever been on.

And it hasn't even begun.

TWELVE

Milo is—

Not a good painter.

We both picked pumpkins and tried to come up with ideas of what to paint. I stuck with something simple and painted the silhouette of a cat surrounded by black music notes. It didn't turn out as bad.

Milo, however, let me decide what he should paint. I told him to paint a self-portrait, but he challenged himself to paint me, and it is a bit insulting.

We walk down the street hiding the monstrosity of a pumpkin that Milo painted, and I'm fighting to keep my laughter to myself even though I'm sure he knows it's not good.

"Are you trying to hide your artwork?" I ask as we move down the street to where the music is playing. Milo's free hand intertwines with my own and I'm surrounded by the easy sounds of the musician strumming on an acoustic guitar and singing slow, sweet music while the festival continues.

"I could never hide your beautiful face." Milo holds the pumpkin out in front of him and displays an odd mix of brown, olive green, and whatever strange color he chose for my shirt. "You're trying to tell me that this isn't a masterpiece? I don't believe it."

I laugh and he tugs my hand closer, brushing my shoulder against his, and I can feel the blush moving up my cheeks.

"You hungry?" he asks, looking over toward the line of food trucks up ahead and past the stage. There isn't a large crowd, so it's easy to move through toward the food where I can see a truck that offers waffles with tons of toppings and options.

"We could get waffles," I offer.

Milo looks up and immediately starts moving toward the stand where the menu shows the options available.

After ordering our food, we find our way to the bleachers across from the stage to watch the musicians that are playing. It's still pretty early, so they are featuring acoustic solo artists, but the guy currently singing is really good.

"I noticed you had a cat when we were back at your apartment," Milo begins. "How long have you had him?"

I swallow the bite of waffle I was working on. "I got him sometime last year. He's supposed to keep me company since I live alone." I don't know if I should tell him I struggled with depression and thought it would be a good idea to get an emotional support animal. Not that Jafar is supportive.

Milo doesn't bring up anything else, so I keep talking. "His name's Jafar.:

He laughs around his food before responding. "Jafar like the villain, Jafar?"

"It suits him," I mutter. "He's kind of an ass."

"Not the company you thought you'd have then, I suppose."

"Definitely not." I smile up at him with the music floating around us. "You'll have to work hard to win his approval. I don't think he even approves of me."

"Well then," Milo starts, "the cat has bad taste. I accept the challenge, though." He leans in a little. "I'm very charming."

I huff a laugh and look back at the stage. A band is now setting up their instruments and preparing for the show.

"Have you ever heard of Curly Fries?" I ask.

"The food?"

"No. It's a band. I actually know some of the members and try to go to all of their local shows. I also fly back to my hometown in Indiana when they play there, too."

Milo pulls out his phone and is typing something into the search bar online. The band members instantly pop up and he turns his screen to face me. "This one?" he asks.

"Yeah, that's them! I think they're playing again next Sunday."

"Ah." Milo raises a brow. "Are you asking me out, Olive?"

I can feel the nerves rush through my body at the statement. Maybe he doesn't want to go out with me again. Maybe he absolutely hates waffles and thinks that was the weirdest choice, especially since they had a pumpkin spice option. What if he thinks I'm absolutely repulsive and the portrait he painted of me is a representation of how he sees me?

"I'd like to go to the concert," I say, my gaze meeting his. I don't dare say anything else.

"Well," he starts, brows furrowed. I can't tell what he's thinking. "If there's an open spot, I'd be happy to go with you."

I sigh a breath of relief. At least he doesn't think I'm completely repulsive. I brush a strand of hair behind my ear. "I'd like that," I say.

~

When we get back to my apartment, I can hear Jafar meowing behind the door where we are standing.

"The infamous villain, Jafar," Milo says. "I think I could probably get him to fall in love with me."

I know he doesn't mean anything by it, but my heart is pounding so fast, and I can hardly look at him. We've had *one* date. That was kind of a weird thing to say. Maybe he feels like his clock is ticking now that he's about to be done with medical school and his residency. Those things keep people busy, and they rarely have time for dating.

"He'll probably try to bite your face off if I introduce you. It wouldn't be a good idea to meet him just yet. I still need to get to know you and haven't decided if you're trying to murder me or not." I finally look back at him, and I watch his eyes flick to my lips briefly. *Oh god.*

I never even figured out if he was in his thirties.

"When's your birthday?" I blurt out.

His face twists in confusion, but there's still a grin on his face. "February third. Why?"

"No, like the year," I add abruptly. *You're being so weird, Olive. He was just about to kiss you and now you're asking him for his year of birth. What are you, the DMV?*

"Are you asking me how old I am?" He smiles, eyes flicking to my lips once more, and my stomach twists. "I'm twenty-seven, Olive."

"Oh." Relief washes over me at that. At least I'm not about to kiss a forty-year-old or something.

"Is that—" The corners of his mouth have dropped, the smile disappearing from his face. "Is that a problem?" he asks.

"God, no!" I squeak, the sound coming out too high to be normal. "I just realized I never asked you."

"Oh."

There's a pause, and I know exactly where this is going. I'm freaking out thinking about everything that happened with Maverick all of a sudden. That boy wasn't in my mind *at all*, but I'm suddenly paranoid. What if I shouldn't kiss him on the first date? Is that too forward?

Before I can finish the thought, his lips are on mine, and it's probably the best kiss I've ever had. *Not that I've had many.*

When he pulls away, I can tell that my face is completely red, and immediately can't get a grip on my nerves.

"Well, goodnight," he says.

"Goodnight," I answer before sliding into my apartment. As soon as the door is closed, I let out a squeal.

Jafar is instantly at my feet, begging for more food. I look at how small he actually is and think about how I'm pretty much on cloud nine.

"Fine, you heathen. Let's get you a second dinner."

THIRTEEN

By the time Thursday rolls around, Milo has been texting me non-stop. I've learned about his parents and his younger sister. I've also learned that he spends his free time reading medical journals, going for morning walks through the city parks, and one other hobby he refused to tell me. He mentioned something about planning another date.

Which means we will have *three.*

I walk out of my apartment building and up to my yellow *Fiat* that has been neglected lately. Tiffany and I made plans to go to lunch after my Ecology and Evolution class was done, and I'm hoping to meet her at a local restaurant in the city.

Phoebe, my car, roars to life, and I'm thankful I won't be taking her into the shop again. The last time she broke down, I was in the middle of a busy intersection.

To say I was freaking out would be an understatement.

When I finally find a spot to park, I lock the car door and walk to the entrance to the restaurant. Before going inside, I send Tiffany a text to ask her if she's here. I notice another message from Milo.

Milo: Had a guy come in with a television remote up his butt.

I cover my mouth as a laugh bursts from my lips. Two customers look at me in confusion, and I apologize and open the door to the restaurant for them. I guess Tiffany is already inside.

Me: Seems like you're getting more experience with things like that. I'm just happy to know I was your first.

I slide my phone into my pocket and spot Tiffany sitting at a table on one side of the restaurant. She's holding her phone, her blonde hair tucked behind her ears.

"Hey," she says as I walk up to the table and pull out a chair. "Why are you smiling?" She gives me a knowing look.

"Milo has been texting me," I admit.

"The doctor?"

I fight off the blush that rises to my cheeks. "Yeah, the doctor. He's supposed to come with me to the Curly Fries show on Sunday."

"Didn't you do that very same date with Gabriel?" Tiffany sips her water through a straw. "Seems a little weird to do the same thing with a different guy."

I scoff at that. "Ridiculous. I'm not going to cease going to concerts with men because I once took a guy to a show, and he then ghosted me for two weeks." I cringe inwardly, feeling guilty. "Well, he didn't really ghost me."

"Right." Tiffany taps the table with a finger. "That entire situation was directly out of a romantic comedy."

I laugh while the waitress comes up to the table. "Except I never got the guy."

"Milo seems promising," she adds with a smile.

"Can I get you guys something?" The waitress asks.

We quickly order our food, including a giant hummus platter complete with pita bread and vegetables.

When our food comes, I grab my phone and see another text from Milo.

Milo: You were not, in fact, the first. I have so many stories from med school.

Something in my chest stings at the thought of Milo having so many others aside from me. It's not that I would judge him, I just don't have the same backlist.

That's a horrible way of phrasing that, Olive.

My heart clenches and I can feel the claws of jealousy sinking into its tender flesh.

I shoot him a text before FaceTime calling Corrine.

Me: Is this a doctor thing or a dating thing?

I hope he doesn't notice how jealous I'm feeling.

It's not like he can see your face.

I tap Corrine's picture on my phone and start the FaceTime call. She picks up quickly, and I can already tell by her face that something stressful has happened.

"Guys," she starts. "I didn't think I would have a phone for this."

I grab a carrot and dip it in the hummus and take a bite. Tiffany is opposite me, looking at the screen I'm holding up between us.

"What happened?" Tiffany asks.

Corrine releases a sigh. "I didn't have my phone all morning! My mom got me a new phone, which was super nice, right? *Wrong.* The transfer did not work. I couldn't make calls on either except to the phone company." She sounds exasperated. "When Brian, the guy with the phone company, asked for my pin, I totally didn't have it. I told him that my line was on my mom's account. Then he tells me to call my mom for the pin!"

"That's ridiculous," Tiffany chimes in.

"I was like, Brian, brother in Christ, that is the exact problem. I don't have a phone and I can only call *you!*"

After hearing about Corrine's phone disaster, Tiffany, Corrine, and I spend the rest of the time talking and eating our food. Corrine asks about Milo, and Tiffany fills her in before I can even explain what's happening.

Before we leave, I hang up the call and see that I have another text message.

Milo: A doctor thing, but I did date.

My heart sinks, and I immediately feel guilty for the reaction. It's not like the guy I date shouldn't have had a girlfriend before me. That would be stupid—especially since Milo is twenty-seven. I would be concerned if he *hadn't* dated anyone.

None of that logic stops my gut from twisting painfully. I'm suddenly nervous as Tiffany and I walk along the sidewalk. He has obviously dated other girls, but what is he going to say when he finds out I've never had sex before? I mean, I had Maverick, but that does not count *at all*.

"Olive?" Tiffany interrupts my thoughts.

"I'm sorry, what?" I look up from my phone and notice we are close to my favorite record store.

"Who is that?" she asks. "Your face is sheet white."

I force a laugh, but it sounds strained. "It's nobody." I gesture to the record store. "We should go in and get Corrine something to soothe the ache of her phone woes."

Tiffany laughs and we open the glass door as bells chime. The whole store smells like incense and soap. It's littered with tourist items, goods that belong in a metaphysical shop, and rows and rows of vinyl records. I stop at the tourist mugs and look for something for Corrine.

My phone dings.

Milo: I'm not dating anyone now though. In case you were worried about that.

I don't answer, picking up a mug that says *let that shit go* and decide I'm going to get it for Corrine. There's also an adult mad-libs game displayed near the mugs. I flip through it and chuckle at the prompts.

My phone goes off again.

Milo: The only date I've been on in the last year is with you.

I smile at that, and another message comes through.

Milo: Not that I'm undesirable. I've just been busy.
Milo: You're not responding. Was it something I said?

I stare at my phone and suddenly feel bad for responding slowly because I feel jealous. It seems juvenile. I glance back at the mad-libs game and decide to pick it up. Maybe we can play it on Sunday after the concert.

Me: No, nothing you said. I was just buying something.

He responds immediately.

Milo: Am I allowed to know what it is?

Me: You'll find out on Sunday.

Milo: Is this supposed to be a spicy text message? Should I say something dirty?

Embarrassment instantly floods my body at his insinuation. I start walking up to the counter with my face on fire and my hand gripped tightly around my phone. I decide to set my two items down and text a response before he makes assumptions.

Me: No!
Me: I mean, no.

Oh god, this is not going well. How can I be so good at embarrassing myself when the guy isn't even around?

Me: It's just a game! No spice.
Me: I have to go.

I can almost hear him laughing on the other side of the phone. I go to the counter and set the game and Corrine's mug on the counter. We lost Tiffany somewhere in the records section and looking for new music.

When the cashier rings up my order, I glance down at my phone one more time. I feel kind of bad for being distracted, but since Tiffany isn't nearby, I go ahead and look at the text.

Milo: See you Sunday, Olive. ;)

Those last two grammatical marks have me instantly freaking out. It's not a spicy text, but it almost feels like it.

I guess I'll find out on Sunday.

FOURTEEN

When the knock sounds on the door, my heart immediately starts trying to break free from behind my rib cage.

I burst from my spot on the couch and bound to the door, twisting the handle and opening it to reveal an incredibly attractive Milo.

I don't know if it's the fact that we've been texting all week, or that he's always been this attractive, but I can't help the way my eyes trail over him.

He's wearing a greenish-blue pair of pants, a black tee, a denim jacket, and black sneakers. I'm surprised to see that he also put a beanie on his head.

"Hey," I say, tucking a strand of hair behind my ear.

"You look nice," he responds.

I peer down at my green turtleneck, black skirt, tights, and thigh-high boots while tugging at the skirt a little.

"Thanks." I offer him a soft smile, and he takes my hand as we walk out of the apartment. I can feel the cool rings he's wearing press against my fingers.

When we get to his car, he opens my door. I get inside the car and quickly fasten my seat belt. Before I know it, we are driving in the direction of the concert.

"So, how do you actually *know* this band again?" Milo breaks the silence, his hand flexing on the steering wheel.

"When they were just starting out, I actually had the band members stay at my family's house back in Indiana."

Milo looks toward me with his brows raised. "You're kidding."

I give a smug smile in return. "Not in the slightest." Looking back at the city passing out the window, I continue. "Their music is good, though. I usually only talk to them at shows now, and we sometimes interact on Twitter."

"Okay." Milo drags out the syllables of the word. I notice his hand tighten on the wheel. "So, I have to win the band's approval?" he asks.

I let out a laugh. "No." I'm looking over at him again, my eyes noticing the slight bump on his nose—as if he had broken it before. "You have to win Jafar's approval," I finally confess. "And that is actually much, much harder."

~

When we get to the concert venue, it hits me.

I absolutely, positively, undoubtedly, and unquestionably have to pee.

I'm standing in line with Milo trying to fight off the urge, but my decision to drink more water and better myself is really not helping at the moment.

Especially since the doors haven't opened yet.

"Is something wrong?" Milo asks while looking down at me. *God, he's tall.*

"No." I scrunch my face, trying to fight the feeling. I literally cannot wait. "I just really have to go to the bathroom."

Olive, you cannot pee yourself on this date.

"Oh," he says, and a small smile appears on his face. "Let's just go up and ask. I don't mind getting out of line, and I'm sure they'd let you in."

We walk up to the box office where a petite woman sits behind the glass.

"Hey," Milo starts, and I'm certain there's no way she can tell us now with how absolutely gorgeous he looks at the moment. "I know the doors aren't open yet, but is there a bathroom she could use?" He nods toward me to show who he's referring to.

I try to plaster on my most charming smile. *Come on, lady. I'm going to explode.*

"Unfortunately, no," she responds. I instantly hate her. "I'm so sorry, but I just can't let you in. There may be a business around here that could let you use the restroom."

"That's fine," I force myself to speak. It is definitely not fine because I am using every ounce of pelvic floor strength to hold back this river.

Milo takes my hand and leads me away from my new arch-nemesis before speaking. "We can look around for somewhere to go."

I want to tell him we can get back in line, but honestly, I'm dying. "Sounds like a plan." I hardly wait for him to start following me before I'm walking off at a swift pace.

Milo is trailing behind me and trying to be helpful as we round the building, hoping to find somewhere—anywhere for me to pee. I can hardly wait for him, but then I feel it.

I stand in the middle of the sidewalk with my legs crossed. Milo is right there in front of me.

"Um," he looks worried. He probably thinks I'm peeing.

"I just need a second," I admit as embarrassment takes over my body. "It'll pass. I'm seriously trying to not pee."

"Right." I can tell he's trying not to laugh.

When the feeling subsides, I take off at a faster pace—practically running around the corner as desperation makes a rapid appearance.

I collide with a body and stumble back before I realize who it is I've run into.

"Joe!" I practically yell. "Can you let me into the building? I have to pee, and they won't let me in."

I think he can see the panic in my eyes. At first, his brow creases with confusion, and then pity washes that expression away. He's with two other band members, Des and John.

"I—" Joe hesitates. "The loading dock is open, but you didn't hear it from me."

"What direction is that in?" I ask.

He points and I take off sprinting, leaving Milo to face the band. I don't hear him behind me, but at this point, I don't even care. I am about to explode.

When I find the loading dock, I sneak in and make my way to the restrooms. I spot Jake setting up the table for merchandise. He recognizes me and says hi. I just wave and keep sprinting to the bathroom.

When I finally get into the stall, I take the most relieving pee of my entire life.

It's only when I wash my hands and walk back out into the lobby to see Jake, I realize that I'm officially the worst date ever.

Where the hell is Milo?

"Olive?" Jake's voice sounds behind me.

"Hey!" I respond. "It's good to see you. Some of the band members told me how to get in after I had a bathroom disaster." I quickly think over what I just said and rush to fix it. "I mean, I didn't have a bathroom disaster!" I correct. "I just had to go incredibly bad."

Shut up, Olive.

Jake laughs a little. "That's fine. Are you coming to the show?"

"Yes, actually." My eyes flick around the large room for Milo. The floors are all solid, beige tile and stretching out into a vast nothingness—not another soul in sight. The doors still aren't open, and I wonder if Milo is still outside. "I am actually missing my date. I better get going."

"That's fine. Good to see you!"

I go back out the way I came in and see Milo standing just outside with his arms crossed. His face looks impassive, and I sincerely hope he isn't pissed, but I can't help but wonder. I did pretty much run away from him and leave him with strangers on only our second date.

"I'm back," I announce, and cringe at my opening line.

"They wouldn't let me go." Milo's brows furrow, and I am instantly afraid he's upset.

"You waited for me." I cross my arms to protect myself against the cool wind that is blowing now that evening is descending on the city.

"No offense," he says, his usual smile returning to his face. Relief instantly washes over me. "Where was I going to go? They wouldn't let me in."

"Right, well, we should probably go get in line."

"Probably." I catch a glimpse of white teeth, and he takes my hand again as we walk back to the entrance. "How's your bladder?"

"Mostly empty," I say, my cheeks flushing as I recall all the events. I'm probably the worst date ever.

Milo's breathy chuckle sounds near my ear as he leans in and places a kiss to my temple. The contact sends chills down my spine.

"Good." The way his low voice rumbles twists my stomach in knots. I can hardly sort it all out. All I know is that I'm attracted to Dr. Jameson, and I'm definitely feeling like things are going well.

"I hope you like the concert," I muse.

"Well," he starts as we make it back to the line. "I've already met the band."

FIFTEEN

Tiffany got to the concert after us, and we hung out as we listened to the band play. Afterward, we even got to talk to the members, and they didn't miss a chance to laugh about my bathroom mishap. When the concert was over, Milo and I drove back to my apartment.

As I open the door, I notice Jafar sprint across the apartment and quickly shove Milo inside while slamming the door closed.

"Sorry," I say. "He tries to escape. I'm pretty sure he thinks I have him imprisoned in hell. Do you have any pets?"

Milo looks around the space, taking in the sheer curtains, wall tapestry, and surrounding plant life. I'm just thankful I cleaned up before the date. It must have been my nerves.

"I don't," he admits while looking back at me. He must read something on my face because he quickly adds, "It's not that I don't like animals. I just don't have the time right now to care for one properly."

"Oh," I say, just as Jafar comes forward and starts weaving through Milo's legs. The cat brushes against his pants and starts purring. It makes me smile. "I guess that didn't take long, huh?"

"I told you I was charming."

My stomach twists and my cheeks heat as Milo stares at me, flashing that smile that makes me melt. There's an awkward pause, and I notice him leaning in. I clear my throat and step away, walking to retrieve the mad-libs game from atop my coffee table.

"I almost forgot!" I blurt as I open the book up. "I found this at the record store the other day and thought it could be fun."

Milo walks over and joins me in sitting on the couch. He takes the booklet from my hands. His touch lingers on mine for a brief moment, and I can feel the way butterflies start swirling in my gut.

When he flips through the book, he looks back at me. "Could be fun, but some of these mad-libs are really inappropriate, Olive."

"Nuh-uh!" I grab the book from him and flip through the different options. I pause on one particular title, a look of horror plastered on my face.

Going Down Right.

Oh. My. God.

Milo clears his throat. "I did ask you if that text was supposed to be spicy. A real missed opportunity, Olive."

"It wasn't supposed to be! I didn't know!" I'm defending myself and completely mortified at the game I suggested we play. Milo doesn't seem bothered by it. In fact, he seems intrigued as he grabs the book from me and looks through other titles.

"We should do one?"

I gulp, remembering the title of the section I just read. "Do what?"

"Fill one of these out. It could be funny."

I just stare at him and something about how his eyes are lighted, and excitement ripples off of him, tells me that maybe it would be fun. I try not to be so ridiculous, straightening my spine.

"Okay," I say. "Let's do it."

~

Half the book later, and over an hour of laughs, Milo and I are sitting on the floor drinking lavender lemonade that I had gotten from the grocery store this past week. We started coming up with categories for our words. We'd say we can only name things in the room or something that could be found in a doctor's office.

The results were hilarious.

Jafar is curled up in Milo's lap on the floor when I close the book and glance at the time. It's two in the morning.

"It's really late," I comment. Milo takes a sip of lemonade and reaches over me to place his glass back on the coffee table.

"I have to work in the morning." He runs his hand over his face, and I can see how tired he must actually be. To be honest, I'm tired too, and I'll have Art History bright and early.

"I had fun today, Olive."

I can't help but notice the way his voice dropped or the way the air is crackling between us. "Me too," I whisper.

The lamp on my end table is emanating dim light through my living room. When a car passes from the street below, headlights stream in my window—muted by the blinds and curtains. The light passes over Milo's face briefly as we stare at one another.

He leans forward, making my heart race so fast I'm afraid I may pass out, but when his lips press to mine, the exact opposite happens. Every nerve in my body is on high alert. I am suddenly aware of every breath—every motion. Especially when Milo deepens the kiss and leans forward. He tastes like lemonade, and all I can think about is the way I'm leaning back and suddenly he's over me on my apartment floor.

Holy shit, this is not *like it was with Maverick.*

Something about this feels different. Maybe it's the fact that Milo didn't come over here with premeditated intentions. Maybe it's the fact that I didn't invite him in some strange attempt at gaining experience. Whatever it is, I can hardly catch my breath when his hand moves under my green sweater.

Milo notices and pulls back. "Is this—" he pauses, looking over me. I notice the way his chest is rising and falling rapidly. "Never mind, I really should go."

"Right," I whisper. My voice sounds defeated, and my chest tightens with the thought that maybe I did something wrong. "Um—" I feel awkward and inexperienced. Milo doesn't look like he wasn't enjoying himself, but if he's trying to leave—

"I want to go out again, Olive." His voice is low as he looks down at me with his hand still on my waist, beneath my shirt. "I don't want you to think that I don't, or that I'm not enjoying myself."

The way he's talking about this has my cheeks on fire. I look over to Jafar, who is now snoozing on the sofa. I feel Milo's thumb brush against my cheek.

"I have to work a lot." His expression is almost pained. "But I really enjoy being around you, and I hope you like being around me, too."

I can hardly breathe. "I like you a lot, Milo."

"Good." He leans down and kisses me once more before standing up straight and grabbing his denim jacket off the floor. He reaches his hand out to help me rise to my feet.

I straighten my skirt before looking back at him. Another car passes and the lights decorate his face. He leans forward and kisses me again, pulling me in at the waist before backing away.

"I don't want to mess this up," he says while drifting toward the door. He keeps going as I smile at him. "I *really* don't want to mess this up right now." I catch the way he looks at me, and my stomach twists.

Is he—?

"I'm going to go now, but I want you to know that I want another date." His hand is on the door, and I chuckle a little. "Like so soon, Olive. I mean it." When the door opens, Milo closes it slowly, about ready to leave. "Next Sunday?" he asks.

"Sure," I say, barely containing the giggle that escapes my swollen lips.

"Okay." The door is almost closed before he bursts back in, rushing forward and kissing me one last time. The force of it is almost bruising.

When he pulls away, he says, "Sunday it is."

And then he's gone.

It only takes a few moments before a text comes through on my phone.

World's Best Pumpkin Painter: I mean it about that date on Sunday.

I laugh at the name he must have added to my phone. It was clearly a reference to the pumpkin he painted during our last date.

Me: I know

World's Best Pumpkin Painter: Thank you for the lemonade.

World's Best Pumpkin Painter: And the kiss.

I bite my lip as I stare at the phone tightly gripped in my hand. It doesn't take long before another message comes through.

World's Best Pumpkin Painter: That was a damn good kiss.

For the first time in my life, I don't feel embarrassed. Before getting ready for bed, I send one more message. I'm so screwed when it comes to class tomorrow. I know I'll be falling asleep during the lecture.

Me: I know.

SIXTEEN

I'm officially exhausted and hardly listening to my Art History lecture—not that it's new or anything.

I keep replaying everything that happened with Milo over and over again in my head. The way he looked at me, the way he—

Never mind.

I glance at my phone, noticing that I have no new notifications. I figured he would text me by now—especially since he asked me to go on another date on Sunday. That never really got confirmed though, and I can't help the painful twisting in my gut—the thing that tells me maybe I got my hopes up again, and Dr. Milo Jameson took a trip to a mental health facility.

Wouldn't be the first time.

As my class comes to a close, the panic starts to crawl its way into my chest—creeping like ivy threatening to choke the very life from my spectacular date.

Maybe the kiss wasn't as good as he said.

In fact, that would be extremely likely, considering that I'd only kissed two men before him. The other problem is that I have no experience. Can men sense things like that? Did he have a sixth sense that clued him in when it came to the fact that I'm a virgin?

Even so, after last night, I'm going to need to tell him and tell him soon. I can't get into a situation where he finds out in the heat of the moment. That's a sure-fire way to get broken up with. Are we even together?

My thoughts are spiraling out of control when the professor dismisses us. I need to go directly to my Contemporary Issues class and as I walk across campus, I finally send him a text message.

Me: What's the plan this Sunday?

I wait, but no response comes through.

My heart drops like lead and a begrudgingly throw myself into a seat, awaiting my demise as the professor enters the room and begins speaking.

Normally, I like this class. Contemporary Issues interest me, but right now, I'm having contemporary issues of my own. I know it's selfish, but after what happened with Gabriel and Maverick, I'm so fearful that things are going to go wrong.

I try to listen to the lecture for the rest of the class. My stomach feels hollow, and I can't decide if it's because I'm hungry, or because I still don't have any text messages from Milo.

I decide to skip going back to my apartment and settle for dining in the cafeteria on campus. The food is absolute garbage, but I don't feel like walking the distance. I'm hoping the gnawing feeling in my stomach is just due to a lack of nutrition.

When I sit down with my food, I realize it isn't. It's definitely because of the notifications that still aren't passing on my phone. I curse myself for being ridiculous and turn my cell phone upside down. I am acting like an obsessive child and need to eat my food. *Stop worrying about Milo.*

I'm just fearful that I'll have to stop thinking about him altogether. It's not so far-fetched with the way my dating life has been going.

"Hey, Olive!"

I groan internally at the familiar voice of Margret. She's standing across from my table, her brown hair looking particularly limp in the cafeteria light.

I roomed with Margo during my freshmen and sophomore years of college at Junesburg, and it was an absolute nightmare.

She was probably the most disgusting human I've ever encountered. And that assessment is not limited to the lack of cleanliness.

She would eat my food, refuse to clean, and talk shit about me behind my back. The entire rooming situation was like living in hell.

No, it was worse than hell.

"Hey, Margret," I say, while poking at the food on my plate.

"Just Margo is fine." She flicks her hair behind her shoulder. I try not to gag. "I heard you were out at a concert last week. Curly Fries, was it? One of my friends saw you there."

I can feel the flush of anger working up to my cheeks. As if dealing with her for two years wasn't bad enough, she's now keeping tabs on me long after I've walked away.

"Oh," I say, trying to school my features into a bored mask. "Yeah." I look down at my plate again and stab a piece of lettuce. *Calm down, the lettuce didn't do anything to you. You don't have to act like you're driving the fork through her throat.*

"Still spending money on concerts but couldn't bother to buy food for the apartment." She flashes a smile and my blood runs cold.

I bought most of the food for the apartment. She would invite her boyfriend over and they would end up eating everything, leaving me to go get more groceries. When I stopped supplying her with food and free cleaning, she started getting mean. That's when she made comments about my love for going to concerts on weekends. They were always targeted at my choices when it came to spending money.

I stare at her ugly face, seething. I don't dare respond to her. Just stab my fork into another piece of lettuce and take a bite. I don't know if she can tell that I'm envisioning her stupid hand beneath the force of my fork.

"Anyway," she continues, oblivious. "Who was the guy? I heard he was hot."

Something about that makes my gut twist again. I still have no idea where I stand with him. I know it hasn't been long, but after last night, I expected something. I would feel better if we confirmed a time. The radio silence is triggering after my experiences with dating.

"Milo?" I ask, flipping my phone and glancing at the lock screen. There are still no messages. I shrug, trying to act unbothered. "He's just a guy I went on a few dates with."

A guy that I really like. A guy that hasn't texted me. A guy that I'm obsessing over. He's just a guy that I can't get out of my stupid head!

"So." Her face scrunches up like she's about to get in a good dig. I brace myself for the rest of her sentence. "Nothing serious?"

My grip tightens on the fork. I'm caught in a weird mix of anger, frustration, and sorrow. I don't know how to react, so I just sit silently for a second before answering. "Not currently, no," I finally grit out.

"Awe." The mock disappointment filling her voice has me seeing red. "Pity. Well, good for you," she says. "Dating and all that."

Margo walks away and I can hardly keep myself from getting up and walking across the cafeteria to shove her face into the table.

My phone finally buzzes, interrupting my thoughts and stopping my heart momentarily.

I carefully flip it over to check the message.

Milo: I'm really sorry. The office has been so busy today, and Dr. Scowls-a-lot is breathing down my neck.

Relief washes over me as I pick up my phone and unlock it when another message comes through.

Milo: Yes, about Sunday. No, to disclosing the surprise.

Milo: It has to do with that hobby of mine. The one you asked about.

I smile at that, thinking of a response to send.

Me: No weird shit, right? You don't dress up in a cloak and pretend to be a wizard on the weekends with a cauldron and everything?

Milo: No cloak for our date. But would it be a problem if I did that?

Oh god. I picture Milo in a dark basement, stirring a pot of green goo and looking wildly around the room as he works on his latest experiment. I can't say I'd be attracted to the cosplay, but the man beneath the cloak definitely does it for me.

Me: I might be able to look past it.

Me: Maybe

I smile when the next message comes through, all thoughts of my earlier encounter with Margo disappearing.

Milo: I mean, I don't pretend to be a wizard on the weekends. I was just wondering.

Milo: Unless you wanted me to. I might consider it then.

My cheeks heat as I stare down at the phone. Is he trying to—

Me: Was that supposed to be spicy?

Milo: Maybe

I snort a laugh, covering my mouth as a few students look up from their tables to stare at me. I give them a half-smile, hoping it's enough to satisfy their curiosity.

Me: I'm thoroughly turned off, Dr. Jameson.

It takes a minute to receive a response, so I eat a few more bites of food, relieved that the hollow feeling in my stomach has disappeared entirely.

My heart skips when I see the next message that comes through.

Milo: See you Sunday, Olive ;)

SEVENTEEN

"Where are we going?"

The brisk air wraps around us as Milo sets a punishing pace along the sidewalk. We had to park on the street—walking to our destination for this date.

I'm still clueless about where we are going. All I know is that I was supposed to dress casually again. This time, something that could get messy. I opted for some cuffed jeans; a tucked-in plain, t-shirt; and a jacket.

"I told you," Milo finally says, glancing back briefly. "It's a surprise."

He is still striding ahead as I fight to keep up with his longer strides. At this rate, I'm going to be jogging at any moment.

"I know you aren't one of the guys I've met in the past on a dating app, but you're really giving off a vibe right now." My voice is unsteady as I follow along, breathing a little harder than I should because of how fast Milo is walking.

Oh my god, what if he thinks I can't keep up? I did tap dancing up through high school. I can't be this out of shape.

Milo turns abruptly and I almost slam into him. I startle, reeling back a bit, but he still has his face so close to mine that I can smell the faintest trace of mint on his breath as it fans over my skin.

"And what vibe is that?" he asks, as if he isn't mere inches from my face. My stomach curls at his closeness.

I swallow hard. "Ax murderer vibes."

Milo raises a brow and cocks his head to the side as he looks at me. "Crazy ax murderer?" he questions. There's a pause before he continues. "You think I'm an ax murderer?" He smiles. "And to think I thought I was just making you burn with desire while your pulse fluttered wildly right—" Milo lifts a finger up and presses it to my neck, feeling where my pulse is. I'm certain it's entirely too fast at this point. I can hardly breathe. "Here," he finishes.

I'm staring up at him with my mouth hanging open. His warm brown eyes gaze down at me, and I can hardly think. The only constant reminder running through my head is that this guy doesn't know that I've never slept with anyone.

The thought makes my stomach twist with nerves.

Milo plants a quick kiss on my lips and chuckles, turning away to keep walking.

"Come on," he says. "We don't have all day."

"Right." My feet are moving rapidly behind him, and my mind is moving just as fast. I can't help but think of all the reasons he wouldn't want to be with a girl like me. He's a doctor, twenty-seven, and has dated before based on his text messages. There's no way of finding out won't be a huge turnoff.

The worst part of it is that I don't want him to decide I'm not worth it. *I'm afraid.*

When we get to two double doors, Milo pushes them open, and I realize I forgot to look for a sign but walking into the airy room lets me know I don't need one. Pottery wheels line the open floor space, and the smell of clay and fire hangs in the air. There are plants decorating the space—giving it a more natural look, along with the hardwood floors and simple décor.

I can't help but smile.

Milo spins around and looks at me from the center of the studio. "Well," he says. "Do you want to learn to make something or not?"

I can feel the smile widen on my face before I offer a response.

Milo is standing expectantly in the center of the floor. The entire studio is empty save for us. I know nothing about pottery, but I am absolutely willing to try.

~

Milo was nothing but kind and patient as he showed me how to center the clay. At first, I had decided to make a vase, but I found that getting the clay tall enough wasn't as easy as it looked. It broke on my first try, and he tried to fix it.

I settled for making a mug, thinking that the shorter the object was, the better chance I had of completing it without looking like a complete buffoon.

I carefully guide the clay, pressing the peddle under the wheel carefully and praying to anyone who will listen that I don't ruin this thing.

Milo is working next to me, and his hands are steady as he shapes the earth like he has been doing this forever.

He probably has.

I realize I'm staring at his hands when my finger breaks through the side of my mug, and I let out a frustrated grunt. Taking my foot off the peddle, I look at Milo, wishing it was as easy as he was making it look.

Milo glances up, watching my dismay, before standing and picking up his stool.

"Here," he says as he places the chair behind me. His legs are on either side of me, and I can feel his warm chest press against my back. Heat washes over me, and I try to remember that we are just making a mug.

Milo moves his hands over mine, guiding me until I'm centering the clay. He leans in to help me work it and keeps guiding me as the mug takes shape again.

I can't focus on anything other than his steady breathing and the way his touch feels on my skin. Even coated in cool earth, it burns.

The mug finally starts to take shape, and Milo pulls his hands away, slowly trailing them over my wrists and tugging to encourage me to let go. I let the peddle slow down a little at a time.

I can feel his chest rising and falling behind me and my pulse speeds up at the contact. I turn my head slightly, watching as his eyes flick down to my lips.

Before I can think better of it, my traitorous brain is mocking me again about my virginal state. Desire is replaced with a kind of nervous fear that is its own all-consuming entity.

I turn away from him, looking at the mug.

"It's still crooked," I say.

Milo stands up, walking around until he's standing just across from me with the pottery wheel between us. He carefully observes the mug, scratching the faint stubble that has appeared on his chin.

"It has character," he finally deduces. I can see the small smile he's holding back.

"So." I wipe my hands on a nearby towel. It does little in the way of cleaning my hands. "What do we do with it now?"

Milo walks over to the sink to clean himself up, his voice echoing across the empty studio when he talks. "Well, Juliette owns the studio. She will throw them into the kiln for us."

My brows furrow at the name. He spoke Juliette's name like they were close friends. I don't know who she is, but jealousy coats my organs like thick honey, making it hard to breathe.

Milo continues. "We can come back and help with the glaze, or you can have her do something simple for you."

My mind is still reeling. "Juliette?" I almost croak.

"Yes." Milo tilts his head slightly as his brows press together on his face as if he didn't understand my statement

A door swings open, followed by the sound of footsteps tapping the studio floor. A tall and beautiful woman with glowing brown skin nearly floats into the room. She's wearing linen overalls covered in paint and clay as she moves right for Milo.

"There's my favorite doctor," she announces while grabbing the sides of his head and planting a kiss firmly on his cheek. "How are you, Milo?"

Bile is rising up my throat, and I have to fight off the urge to throw up. *This is way worse than an ax murderer.*

"Lillian," Milo begins.

Okay, so not Juliette. How many women does this guy have?

He continues. "This is Olive. Olive, this is Lillian." He's gesturing between us and I fight to keep my face neutral. "Lillian is Juliette's wife," he supplies.

The guilt I feel is instant.

You're such a jealous idiot!

"Hello," I say, offering not Juliette but her wife, a soft smile. I reach out to shake her hand, but she bats mine away.

"Oh, none of that," she chides, going in for a hug. My arms feel stiff, but I hug her back.

When she pulls away, Lillian pats my cheek, and I catch a whiff of her floral perfume. "Ah," she says before holding me by the shoulders and looking me over. "You're the girl" There's a short pause. "Pretty thing, this one. I see why you've become so taken with her, Milo."

I swear I see pink staining Milo's cheek as he clears his throat. "Thank you for letting us use the studio." He gestures to the room as if Lillian didn't know what he was talking about. He seems flustered by her comment, and I can't help but smile.

"Not a problem, dear." Lillian releases me and strides over to the cabinets at the far end. She opens them and starts digging around. "Just as long as you were minding the cameras." She flicks a sharp gaze over her shoulder and smiles brightly. "We aren't trying to make those kinds of movies in this place if you know what I mean."

Lillian winks at me, and I instantly want to drown—or be buried. It doesn't matter the method, I'm ready to disappear.

Just let me die peacefully.

"Well," Lillian begins again, turning to face us. Milo is now standing next to me, and I can still see the slightest shade of pink decorating the slightly tanned skin on his face.

I really need to ask if he goes tanning. I still need to ask about the butthole thing.

"The night is young." Lillian claps her hands together once. "I suspect you're still taking sweet Olive to dinner. Right, Milo?"

Milo runs a hand through his hair, smearing the smallest bit of clay in the brunette strands. "Yes, of course." He's fumbling for words, a stance, *anything.*

It helps me relax a little, seeing him so flustered.

Milo reaches for my hand as we move toward the doors of the studio.

"Come back and see us soon!" Lillian calls.

We are walking back to the car at a much slower pace and the smallest piece of guilt returns. "Wife," I mutter under my breath.

"What?" Milo asks.

Heat rises to my cheeks. "Oh," I say a little louder. "Nothing."

There's an unspoken tension in the air as I continue spiraling down the rabbit hole of all the ways my virginal state could be utterly repulsive to the man walking next to me.

For starters, he may judge me for how old I am. Then there's the issue of him thinking I'll become clingy. Nobody wants to be someone's first time if they think they will become a blood-sucking leech—never breaking off the connection because they feel bonded. That isn't me, but he doesn't know that.

Milo opens the car door and we both get in. The silence is like a curse, weighing heavily on my shoulders.

"I'm a virgin!" I blurt out, slapping my hand over my mouth. I manage to sneak one look at Milo to realize he's staring at me wide-eyed, and now I'm mortified.

Please let the good Lord take me. Any deity really.

"I thought you should know," I continue, fidgeting with my hands in my lap. "Considering what Lillian was saying. I just—" I don't know how to say it. There's a part of me that wants to cry, but I manage to shove down the tears as my brows furrow. "I just thought you should know."

Milo is just staring at me still and the silence is killing me. I can't handle it, so I close my eyes and let my head gently rest against the seatback behind me.

I can't stop talking then. "And I understand if you're not wanting to be with me anymore. You're *twenty-seven*. There's no way you are too, and honestly, I wouldn't expect that or care. In fact, it would be weird. I just felt guilty after that kiss the last time." I sigh, opening my eyes and staring out the front windshield of Milo's car. "That *was* a damn good kiss. At least for me."

I bite my lip, willing myself not to cry. Milo still isn't saying anything, so I push on.

"I knew I needed to tell you, but I was having such a great time on our date." I finally turn to look at him. "And then Lillian walked in, and I was suddenly jealous and—"

"You were jealous?" he asks, eyes widening.

"Not the point," I grunt, looking away. "I am freaking out about this because who wants to be the first, right? Not that I don't want to. Especially after everything, but you're going to think I will become way too attached and clingy, and nobody wants something like that."

Milo's brows furrow. "You want to have sex with me?"

I ignore him. "And *nobody* wants someone clingy and bound to them like that. This is probably the most I've ever talked about this." I finally look at him again, but I can't read his expression through my spiraling thoughts. "I didn't say anything sooner because I really like you and I didn't want to—"

My words are cut off by a kiss. Milo's lips are on mine in an instant, his fingers threaded in my hair.

When he pulls back, I whisper, "Mess this up."

I can see a small smile stretch across his face. "You're not messing anything up, Olive. It's fine." He kisses me again, and something like relief washes over me.

"Okay," I say against his lips.

"Okay." Milo's smile widens as he pulls away. He turns on the car and starts driving to wherever he is planning to take me next.

There is a companionable silence, but my nerves are slowly settling.

That went better than I thought.

"So," he breaks the quiet. "You want to have sex with me?"

I look over to see the wide smile breaking his face and embarrassment creeps up my neck to my face.

I don't respond at first and glance out the passenger window, hoping to find the right words. "I mean, things are going well." *Someone help me.* "I don't know what I'm saying," I finish.

"It's just funny," Milo says, his fingers stretching out from where he grips the steering wheel.

"What's funny?" I ask. My gut feels like there's lead there, holding me down and creating a sick feeling in my stomach.

"How nervous and flustered you are about this." He glances sideways at me. "It's not like I haven't already been up there."

"That was different," I defend.

"It was."

There's another short silence.

"Can we talk about something else?" I ask, trying to avoid the subject of sex with Milo. I don't think my thoughts, or my body can handle that right now.

"You were jealous," he says.

Not much better!

I throw my hands in the air. "I didn't know they were lesbians!" I run my hand down my face. "I thought you had a secret girlfriend, or wife, or harem. I don't know!"

Milo chuckles. "They're good friends—Juliette and Lillian. Juliette and I met during my undergrad. She was planning to go to med school but chose the studio instead. I'm pretty sure Lillian convinced her it would be okay. Juliette is hard on herself; it was hard for her to quit."

"Is she happy?" I ask. "With the studio, I mean."

"Yeah, I think so." Milo pulls into a parking spot and puts the car into park.

When he turns and smiles at me, my heart nearly skips a beat.

"I hope you're hungry."

EIGHTEEN

Milo took me to a small café overlooking the city lights, highlighting the now damp street. I was starving, and thankful for the break from our awkward conversation in the car.

"So," I start, "I don't know a lot about your family."

Milo finishes chewing a piece of food before answering my question. "No traumatic past for me," he says. "It really messed up the entire brooding bad boy persona I was trying to go for."

I can hear the sarcasm dripping from his tone and snort a laugh, covering my mouth quickly.

"My parents are from here," he continues. "They live in Colorado now, though." A smile crosses his face and my heart stutters in response. "I know what you're thinking, and no, they don't sit around smoking pot all day."

I chuckle as I take another bite of food. "What about siblings?" I ask.

"A younger sister." Milo sits back and brings the glass of water to his lips. My eyes catch there, and I see the corner of his mouth pull up when he notices. "She was a bit of a surprise. She's only fifteen."

The waitress walks up and asks us if we need anything. We politely decline.

I bite my lip, thinking about the way Milo's hands were on me as we molded the mug earlier. "Pottery is an interesting hobby for a doctor. Do you have any others?" I'm desperately trying to keep him from noticing where my thoughts went.

"Plenty," he says, smiling behind his glass of water again.

When the waitress comes back around, Milo asks for the check, and I glance around the quiet restaurant.

Looking to the door, I spot a familiar form, and I'm fairly certain all of my internal organs shut down.

"Oh, shit," I whisper.

Milo's head whips around. *Very discrete.* He catches sight of who walked in.

Gabriel is talking to the hostess, and it looks like he is waiting to get a table. Just then, he starts walking in our direction, and Milo turns around and points a thumb toward the door.

"Is that the guy from the supermarket?" he asks.

I want a wide abyss to open up beneath me and get me out of this absolute hellscape. "Yes," I groan, covering my face with my arms.

When I look up again, it's just in time to hear Milo say, "Don't look now." Gabriel's eyes meet mine, and he's suddenly standing next to our table, glancing down at me.

"Hey, Olive," he says. I can't help but catch the jittering nerves laced in his tone.

Internally, I am screaming, but I try to remain calm on the outside. "Hey, Gabriel. How are you?"

Gabriel gives a soft smile before answering. "Pretty good." He glances toward Milo. I don't know if he recognizes him from the day he told me why he ghosted me, but I sincerely hope he has no clue. "Oh," Gabriel says, brows furrowing. "I didn't realize you were—"

"On a date?" Milo finishes for him with one brow raised.

"Sorry." Gabriel quickly composes himself, pretending that he wasn't just flustered. "I'm glad everything is going well for you." He smiles again, and I almost believe it. "I'll see you around, Olive."

When he walks away, it feels like the oxygen returns to the room.

"Thank god," I huff, dropping my forehead onto my arm on the table.

"He's devastated," Milo says, and I can hear the humor in his voice.

Looking up, I see I was correct about the humor. Whatever devastation Milo sees in Gabriel amuses him. Unfortunately, based on what the boy told me about a month ago, he's probably right.

"You have no idea," I mutter, looking back to where Gabriel is now scooting into a booth and smiling up at the waitress. I can see it then, how the smile doesn't quite reach his eyes, and my gut twists painfully.

"Missing out on you really did him in, huh?" Milo's voice draws me from my thoughts. I look back at him, registering what he said and smiling.

"I don't think I had anything to do with it," I say.

Milo leans in a bit, his voice dropping low. "I don't see how you couldn't. I'd be devastated to see you with another man after I had my chance."

My stomach flutters, and the waitress comes over with our check.

~

The car ride is silent for the first few minutes as a never-ending stream of city lights passes by my window. I feel Milo's hand resting on my thigh, and I can hardly think past that simple touch. It's almost like his skin is burning right through me.

"Do you want to watch a movie?" Milo asks, breaking my less than pure thoughts.

I look over at him in the driver's seat, his hand still a gentle weight on my leg. "That sounds good," I say.

He clears his throat as if he's uncomfortable. "We could go back to my house," he suggests. "I have popcorn. The movie is your choice."

I think back to the last time I was alone with a man watching a movie, and how awful it felt.

Well, it wasn't awful, necessarily. It was just not the right man.

I wonder if maybe Milo would be more willing to watch my favorite movie than Maverick was. If he makes it through the entire thing, I have to deduce that his intentions are nothing but noble.

Though you did pretty much tell him you want to have sex with him, Olive.

I cringe at the thought.

"What do you think about *Mamma Mia!?*" I ask.

Milo flashes his white teeth, and there is something so genuine about the way he smiles. It's as if he means every single one. "If you're excited about it, then so am I."

~

Milo walks me up the brick walkway leading to his house. My eyes are wandering over the brickwork, and dark wooden accents. The entire place screams old Tudor cottage with a modern twist.

When the red front door opens, I take in the clean space. Black and white photographs of beautiful landscapes hang on the walls and a television is mounted above a fireplace. At the back of the living room are black bookshelves with various titles stretched from side to side.

Milo walks in and turns back.

"I'll be back," he says. "I'm just going to use the restroom and make some popcorn. Make yourself at home."

I walk over to the bookshelves, running my fingertips along the medical textbooks and journals I find there. The scent of vanilla invades my senses.

When I hear Milo's shoes tap the hardwood, I don't bother turning around. "I'm surprised you don't have a cauldron in here." I'm smiling when I spin to see him standing by the coffee table with a giant bowl of popcorn.

"I told you," he starts, setting the bowl on the wooden surface. "I was willing to remedy that situation. All you have to do is ask."

I let out a breathy chuckle and move to sit next to him on the couch.

Milo places his arm around me seamlessly and finds *Mamma Mia!*, and displays it on the screen.

Then, the craziest thing happens.

Milo watches the entire movie with me, commenting on the plot and refusing to balk as I gush about my favorite scenes.

When the screen goes dark, I'm curled up with my legs on the couch and my head on his chest, desperately wishing I could stay here forever.

"I should probably get going." I sit up, and Milo unwinds his arm from around my shoulders.

I gather my jacket from the arm of the couch and walk to the red door where Milo follows me. When I turn to say goodbye, my breath catches at the heated look in his eyes.

Milo slowly raises his hand and touches a piece of my hair, dragging his fingers down the strands.

His mouth tips up at one end. "Clay," he says. There's something darker in the way he's speaking, and I fight to keep my hormones in check.

He made it through the entire movie. He's a noble guy.

The only problem is that I can feel my own nobility slipping through my fingers. I don't dare ponder what that means for me.

I let out a tight laugh, hoping he doesn't notice how fast my heart is beating. "That mug better be worth it, then."

Milo is still wearing that crooked grin, and I am practically melting into a pile of goo on the floor. "I just hope it can stand up straight. It looked pretty drunk."

There's a moment of silence where I feel everything crackling between us. I have no idea what's happening. I just know that Milo is looking at my lips and moving forward, and I don't think I've wanted anything more in my life.

When his lips press against mine, I'm almost breathless. All I can think about is that vanilla scent and freshly fallen snow in the winter. The way it glitters and coats the earth with a subtle peace.

Then something happens that I didn't expect. All of that snow melts, replaced with something like fire.

I can feel every nerve in my body as Milo pushes me against the door. I'm fighting for air still, and when his hand trails over my torso, a small noise escapes my lips.

Cue the embarrassment.

Milo pulls back when I stiffen.

"I—" I'm struggling for words. "I should go," I finally say. It's not that I don't want things to continue, I just—I have no idea. I don't want to move too fast.

Milo steps back and runs a hand through his hair. He looks flustered and flushed, his lips swollen. "Right," he stutters. "Of course."

I step forward and place a small kiss on his lips before pulling back, desperate to let him know that I'm not disinterested.

"I want to take you out again," he finally says when I step back toward the door. "Next weekend I'm going home. It's an early Thanksgiving with my family—the only time they could do it. They got a deal on a cruise for the actual holiday."

My stomach twists with disappointment. "That following week, I'll be back in Indiana for the real holiday."

I didn't know something could sting so badly. Maybe I'm making a mistake by leaving here. Maybe I should stay and see where this goes.

You know exactly where it would go, Olive. You've only just confessed to him you've never slept with someone before. You need to make sure he really processes that. If he's going to run, give him a chance to do it.

Sorrow burns like a bitch.

"Right," he says, looking almost as dejected as I feel.

I clear my throat. "Well, Goodnight."

Twisting the door handle and allowing the wood to creak as fresh air winds its way into the room, I can't help the nagging of the sorrow building in my chest. I need to do something.

I spin around abruptly. "You should come," I say, nerves wracking my body.

"What?" he asks, eyebrows flicking up.

Goddamn. Way to make this harder. I'm using all the courage I own for this.

"To my family's Thanksgiving," I clarify. "You know, if you're not doing anything."

He doesn't answer, and I know I've messed up. My heart plummets into my stomach, sending it twisting with all the food I don't want to release onto the carpet.

"Was that too soon?" I ask, wincing.

"No. I just—" I can't tell what he's thinking. "You're serious."

God, Olive! How do you do damage control now? Act aloof.

"Yeah, I guess." I can't look him in the eyes. There's no way I want to see what he's thinking. I don't want to know what is crossing his mind right now. Milo probably thinks I'm insane for asking him to my family's Thanksgiving after what, three dates?

"Okay," he says, and my eyes snap up and catch on his own. "Thanksgiving it is, then. Are we booking a flight?"

"Yeah, I mean, I can make some adjustments." I'm stuttering. *I can't believe he agreed to this.*

I smile, unable to contain my excitement. "Goodnight, Milo," I finally say, turning to open the door again.

"Goodnight, Olive."

NINETEEN

My mother's squeal of excitement startled Jafar from his spot on the couch when I told her about Milo coming for Thanksgiving over FaceTime. It's only been three days since my date with Milo, but he seems intent on coming.

"Finally," she huffed.

I couldn't help feeling a little irritated at that. Keeping my face a bored mask, I respond. "I haven't been on many dates with him yet, mom."

She rolls her eyes. "Yes, but it seems like it's going well!"

"It is."

"Is he going to do a PowerPoint presentation? I think that would be hilarious." My mom is smiling through the phone.

I hadn't considered telling him, but it is an important tradition. Each year, my family creates and presents stupid PowerPoint presentations. Last year, Jo matchmade the entire family with *Disney* princesses and princes.

I have to admit; it was pretty funny.

"I mean, maybe I can tell him about it. I don't know if he will make one, though." I didn't want to throw him under the bus.

I minimize the FaceTime call and quickly type out a text message to Milo.

Me: Strange request . . .

I pull the FaceTime call back up and listen to my mom talk about what is going on back in Indiana. I have to admit I miss them.

When Jafar jumps back up on the couch, I reach my hand out and pet him, trying to seek comfort and praying to any god that will listen that he doesn't come for me and try to bite me.

After an hour of talking, I hang up with my mom and hop in the shower before meeting Tiffany for dinner. I haven't spent nearly as much time with her as I would like. During the week, my classes have really picked up since we are nearing finals, and I have been spending most Sundays with Milo.

My stomach twists at the thought of not seeing him this coming weekend, but it's important for him to see his family, too.

I lean my head back and relish in the hot water running over my skin. Something about it eases the ache of two weeks without Milo.

Stop being ridiculous, Olive. You hardly know the man.

When the water stops flowing, I wring my hair out and pull a towel around myself while I hear the buzzing noise my phone makes from atop the counter.

Jumping out of the shower, I quickly check it for a response. Tiffany asked about dinner, and I shoot her a text confirming that I still plan to be there. Then I see the text from Milo.

Milo: Does it involve a cauldron?

I snort aloud, making Jafar skitter from the bathroom. I shout over my shoulder. "Shouldn't have been in here to begin with, you perv!"

Me: No cauldron. Well, maybe.
Me: My family has this tradition where we create stupid PowerPoint presentations and share them on Thanksgiving. It could literally be about anything. Last year, my cousin rated the ex-boyfriends of some celebrity. I wanted to know if you wanted in on the game.

I comb my hair out and go searching for an outfit.

Jafar is curled up on my bed, and I pet him before moving to my mostly clean clothing pile. "You're not really a pervert, Jafar." I coo. He tries to nip my finger. "Ouch! I take it back, asshole."

Picking up my phone again, I read the response.

Milo: Of course I want in.

I stare at the message, my stomach flipping wildly. I can't help but think about—

Milo: Poor wording. I would love to make a PowerPoint. Is this a competition, because if so, good luck.

Me: Don't worry. I'm a professional since I'm the one that started the tradition. I don't need luck.

Once I'm fully dressed and made-up, I slide on a pair of shoes and make my way out the door, making sure I turn to Jafar before leaving. "Be good. Don't die."

I lock up my apartment and walk down the steps.

~

"Against the door?" Tiffany is practically shouting in the restaurant, and I reach a finger up to shush her.

Excitement is practically rolling off her and has been since I've updated her on almost everything that has happened between myself and Milo.

"It wasn't anything crazy," I say, tasting the lie on my tongue. *It was absolutely crazy for you, Olive.* "I left afterward."

"Girl, you should have stayed."

I sigh and lean back in the restaurant chair, tapping a finger on the wooden surface of the table.

"I have to come up with a PowerPoint for Thanksgiving. I told you about that, right?" I lean forward to grab my water and take a sip. "Milo is going to make one too."

"Things are getting serious if he's making entire PowerPoint presentations for you."

I chuckle at that as the waitress comes and leaves our bill. Milo has been treating me to meals every Sunday, so I decided to pay for Tiffany. I have a little extra cash to spare. Besides, Tiffany is taking Jafar for Thanksgiving.

"You're sure you don't mind having Jafar with you?"

"You're kidding?" she asks. "Of course, I don't mind! He may be Satan himself, but he's awful cute."

"That's probably true."

Tiffany and I walk out of the restaurant together, following the sidewalk and window shopping at the cute boutiques on this strip.

My eyes catch on a dinosaur shirt made for a toddler, and I instantly think of Elias. I will get to see him soon, so I tug on Tiffany's arm and convince her to go in.

After buying the shirt, I say goodbye and walk down to where I parked my car to get in.

Milo: What's the sleeping situation over Thanksgiving?

My face is red. I'm sitting alone in my tiny yellow car with a complete blush on my face. It's utterly ridiculous. I don't know exactly what to say, but Milo already bought whole plane tickets to visit Indiana with me. There's no way I'm making him buy a hotel room, too.

Me: You can stay at my parents if you want.

I don't dare say anything more than that. I have a pretty good idea that he's thinking we will share a room, and honestly, I don't mind.

There is still a part of me that feels weird about sharing that space with my parents sleeping in the house. Especially since Milo and I haven't gotten that far in our relationship.

Milo: Sounds good. I'll sleep anywhere. ;)

I fidget with the tear in my jeans nervously before starting my car. My mind fills with a million different thoughts—most including Milo and I in compromising positions.

I should feel guilty about it, but I absolutely do not.

Me: Honestly, same. ;)

TWENTY

The two weeks without Milo went by faster than I imagined, the ache being eased by the fact that we were on the same flight and Milo held my hand the entire way, asking me endless questions about my family and what to expect.

If I didn't know any better, I would have thought he was nervous. Honestly, I have more of a right to be nervous. I love my family, but they're a bit of a mess.

We had rented a car at the airport. I didn't want my mom picking us up and making Milo feel like he was stuck or bound to me like some kind of prison sentence. I don't think he minded, though.

We parked at the foot of the driveway since my parents live on top of a monstrous hill. It's absolutely ridiculous how steep the walk up is from down below, but with my grandparents being older, and my grandfather being sick, it's important that they got to park up by the house.

I'm trying desperately to hide how hard I'm panting as I keep pace with Milo.

"You weren't kidding about this damn driveway," he says.

Somehow, I don't believe he's affected at all. He's breathing evenly, and I'm struggling to respond to his ridiculous statement. "What are you, a superhero? You're not even breathing heavily." I try to keep my voice steady. "I know I'm not the most athletic person in the world, but I danced growing up. I don't understand how you're doing this so easily."

He glances over his shoulder, his gaze searing as it trails over my body. "You're fine," he says. "Though I will say this steep hill explains your ass."

I stop walking, completely stunned at the comment. It's not that Milo hasn't flirted with me; it's just never been so—outright.

He pauses and turns around, leaning back slightly to counteract gravity. "Did I say something wrong?" He's frowning, his black and gray sweater pulling tight across his chest. I try not to look and fail.

"No, I just haven't heard you talk like that." I waltz ahead and the driveway levels out as we make it up to the set of stairs that go to the door of our brick ranch-style home. I can tell my dad had put effort into the decorating this year. There's a giant metal sign with a turkey on it in the yard.

Milo trails behind me. "Ah, a better view," he comments, and my cheeks heat.

When we get to the door, he's standing next to me, that vanilla scent from his house invading my lungs and making my mind dizzy.

Looking over at him, I notice the wide smile on his face. He threads his fingers through mine and winks. "Though it's not the only admirable feature you have."

"My intelligence has to be one," I mutter.

There's a wicked glint in his eyes. "Only second to your boobs."

The door opens before I can get an answer out. I'm gaping like a fish as my mom pulls my—whatever he may be into a tight hug. I can tell she's excited and completely unaware of what he just vocalized.

I can't say I didn't like it.

~

Milo doesn't balk at my family. He's quick to converse with my mother and grandmother, quick to play with my nephew, Elias, and eager to get to know everyone who showed up for dinner.

I watch as he pulls out the dinosaur t-shirt that I bought Elias over a week ago and gives it to him. My nephew is practically shaking with excitement, and I'm pretty sure my heart has melted into a puddle on the floor.

The only difficult part of dinner is that I notice how sick my grandfather really is. It wasn't anyone's fault, they probably don't notice as much being here all the time, but when I'm in a different state for long stretches, it is a bit of a shock to come back and see how frail he's gotten.

I pick at my food, glancing at the version of my grandfather that I never wanted to become a reality. His skin is pale, and he looks so thin. His voice has developed a rasp showing his age, and my chest squeezes tightly.

I look around the room, knowing that it must bother my other family members as much as it bothers me. The only difference is they are here with him. I'm off getting my degree and missing the little time we have left.

When I excuse myself to go to the bathroom, I can feel the tears working behind my eyes. I try to daub them away before walking out, but I know someone will notice how bothered I am.

"Are you okay?" Milo catches my elbow in the hallway as soon as I exit the wooden door.

"I'm fine," I say, trying not to be an emotional mess.

Milo leans down, placing his hands on my shoulders and trying to meet me at eye level. He's much taller, so the task is difficult. "Something's wrong," he remarks.

"I just—"

I just feel completely ridiculous because nobody told me. Nobody told me how things would be and there's a sorrow settling over the room at how sick he is. I feel selfish for not thinking of him more. I feel selfish for not being here.

A tear spills down my cheek, and Milo gently wipes it away with the pad of his thumb. His touch is warm, and I'm desperately fighting off the breakdown. "Talk to me," he whispers.

"My grandfather's sick."

"I know," he acknowledges. "You told me about the cancer before we came." His brown eyes are searching mine, trying to find an answer to why I'm so sad.

"I just didn't realize how bad he had gotten." My voice is hardly audible as I look away, scrubbing another tear from my face. "It's hard to be away and then come back to realize how much I've missed and how little time we may have with him." The tears are really flowing now. "It makes me feel selfish for being at school."

"You're not selfish, Olive." Milo's voice is gentle. "Just because hard things are happening doesn't mean you're supposed to feel pain every minute of every day."

He pulls me closer, running his hand down my hair. I can't help it, and it seems so ridiculous, but something about the way he's holding me has me suddenly sobbing and shaking with the weight of it all.

Milo doesn't move, he just lets me cry, not forcing me to hurry back to dinner. At this point, I don't care what my family thinks we are doing.

When the tears run dry, and I finally pull away, my heart nearly shatters at the concern filling Milo's face. I honestly don't know how he can be so caring when we've really only known each other for three months.

I chuckle, looking at the sweater Milo is wearing. There's a huge wet spot on his chest where I was burying my face moments ago. "I'm sorry about that," I say, pointing to the darkened circle.

Milo shrugs, a smile appearing on his face. "What good are clothes for but to mop up the tears of beautiful women?"

I laugh again. "That was kind of cheesy."

His lips meet mine, gentle and cool against my mouth.

When he pulls away, he's smiling again. "We should go back out there before they think we are doing something suspicious."

"Like sobbing in a hallway?"

I can see the amusement in his eyes before he speaks. "Like fucking in a bathroom."

My cheeks heat, and I can't even look at him. The embarrassment races through my body at an alarming pace.

"Right," I say, but my voice is almost a squeak. Milo laughs, and the low sound has heat washing over me for a different reason. "It's almost PowerPoint time, anyway."

"Of course!" he says. "I'm going to apologize now. Just because you are sad doesn't mean that I won't completely wipe the floor with you in this competition."

A corner of my mouth turns up. "I wouldn't expect anything less."

~

I make it through my presentation where I rate each former United States president based on how hot I think they are without completely falling apart laughing.

Milo sat on the couch next to Jo, cackling the entire time.

When it was his turn, I realize that he actually went all out for his presentation. It was called *Reasons Why Olive Should Stop Calling Jafar an Asshole*. The entire presentation consisted of the cutest pictures of my cat ripped off my social media.

I have to admit; it was pretty good.

When we finished the presentations, we got out an adult card game and rope my grandmother into playing. She always likes to pretend that she's some noble god-fearing woman, but she's actually the raunchiest of us all.

By the time we are getting close to the end of the game, everyone can hardly breathe from laughing so much. I notice my grandmother is laughing the hardest, especially when Milo keeps putting in the dirtiest cards.

"I can't believe you put in a card about an orgy!" I whisper, scolding him while people are choosing their cards.

Milo shrugs. "I mean, it was a good pick. I don't care if your brother Harold was choosing, or if your grandmother was listening." He leans in and I can feel his breath fan over my neck as he whispers. "I'm here to win."

Tension crackles, but I do my best to shove it down when my grandmother reads off the answer choices.

"What is the best way to woo a woman?" she reads, holding up the prompt card.

"Mine is definitely going to win," Milo whispers.

"Going in the back door," my grandmother reads while her features morph into an expression filled with disgust. "Oh, gross, guys," she says, but I can tell she finds it just as funny as the rest of us.

It isn't long before she's reading the next response, and I can tell by the look on Milo's face that it's his card. "Viagra," my grandmother reads.

I don't think I've ever heard her laugh so hard in my life. We are all joining in, but I can't tell if I'm laughing at the card or my grandmother.

Just when I think things are going well, the literal worst thing happens.

My grandmother laughs so hard, and before I know it, vomit is spewing out of her mouth and onto the table.

The laughter instantly subsides.

"Oh my god," she says, covering her mouth while my parents and aunt rush around for things to clean up. "I laughed so hard I puked."

She doesn't appear sick beyond the huge mess and awful smell.

Milo lets out a soft chuckle and walks around, trying to help my family get her all cleaned up.

I don't know who is more mortified, myself, or my grandmother.

When everything finally settles, we decide to put the game away, and since it's getting late, people are finally taking off.

As the house clears out, Milo goes down to the rental car to retrieve our bags.

When he gets back up, my dad is helping my mother clean up in the kitchen. We are standing at the kitchen's entrance, the red walls illuminated with the fancy light fixture my mom has hanging from the ceiling. I'm fairly certain the chrome object was here before we moved in, but I can't remember.

"Milo," my dad says. "You're welcome to the guest room."

Milo glances at me, and I don't know how to react. Does he expect me to sleep with him?

Oh god, he probably does!

"That sounds great," he finally says brightly.

"Don't worry about him," my mother chimes in, patting Milo on the shoulder. "You can sleep wherever you want."

My mom is looking at me like she did me a giant favor. Embarrassment grips me like a vise, and I let a weak smile show on my face.

Milo must read my expression because he says, "The guest bedroom is just fine. I will go drop off my things."

With that, I breathe a sigh of relief. I don't know if I can handle my first time being in my childhood bedroom. Something about it makes me cringe.

TWENTY-ONE

I can hear the clock ticking as I toss and turn in my childhood bedroom. Old band posters littered the walls, and clothes are strewn across the floor. I really should have cleaned up the last time I was here.

Turning onto my side, I can't help but thinking what Milo is doing. Glancing at the clock, I notice it reads two-thirty in the morning.

He's most likely sleeping.

I can feel how dry my throat feels, like sand is coating my entire esophagus. It's one more reason I can't get settled, so I huff and throw the blankets off of my legs.

Crawling out of bed, I make my way up the stairs and to the kitchen for a glass of water.

Sometime after my brother Harold moved out, I moved down into the basement. The nice part of it is that there's a bathroom, and a separate living area complete with a fireplace. The bad part is that the kitchen is on the second floor.

When I reach the top of the steps, my body slams into something massive.

Milo catches me as I almost tumble back down to the depths of the basement.

"Hey," he whispers. The stove light gives me the slightest glimpse of his face. He's wearing gray sweatpants and a fitted white shirt. His hair is mussed as if he were just in bed.

Duh, Olive! He was just in bed.

"What are you doing up?" I ask.

I can see the faintest tint of pink on his cheeks in the dim lights. "I was trying to find the bathroom."

"Right," I say, still speaking in hushed tones. "It's back down the hallway. Here."

I walk him to the bathroom and return to the kitchen to open the white cabinet for a glass.

The fridge gurgles as I fill my glass with water, and I cringe, hoping to not wake anyone up in the middle of the night.

The cool water sooths my dry throat before I walk to the sink to discard the dish.

I hear footsteps enter the kitchen behind me. Turning to see Milo, I offer a soft smile, leaning back against the countertops with my hands resting on the edge.

"I can't believe your grandmother laughed so hard she threw up," he whispers.

I tuck a strand of hair behind my ear. "Yeah. The worst part is that it isn't a new event. She actually does stuff like that a lot. It's not surprising you got to be here for all the action."

"I really thought something was wrong," he admits. "I thought I was going to have to go all Dr. Jameson on her and save the day. It's really a bad look now that I didn't get to do that." He runs a hand through his already mussed hair and continues talking in a low tone. "If I had done that, I'm pretty sure you wouldn't have been able to keep your hands off me."

A twinge of guilt stabs my gut. "Are you disappointed?"

He tilts his head in confusion. "Disappointed at what?"

"Disappointed that we didn't sleep in the same room. I thought it might be weird, especially since I don't know what we are right now." I hate how insecure the last statement comes out sounding.

"What do you want to be?" he asks, his voice thick with something I can't quite figure out.

"I don't know." I can feel the nerves working their way through my body. I don't really know if this is an appropriate time for this conversation, anyway. "Definitely not a doctor and a patient," I supply, avoiding answering what I actually want.

Milo steps forward until he's inches from my face, running his fingers gently along my cheek. I can see humor dancing behind his brown eyes. "You mean you didn't enjoy being my patient?" Milo leans in and that scent of vanilla wraps around me. I can feel my entire body coming alive with his proximity and the way his breath ghosts over my lips. He's leaning so close, sending my heart pounding in my chest. 'You didn't enjoy having my fingers inside of you?"

My breath catches as my eyes meet his, and I'm barely able to function beyond the desire I see there. I can't really see beyond the hormones that are slowly taking control of my body either. "That was for medical purposes." I try to sound unaffected and logical, but I don't think it comes out that way.

"Ah," he says smoothly, leaning back. "You're right." He winks at me. "Not the same thing."

There's a question hanging in the air between us. The darkness outside begging me to answer. I'm not sure what I want. All I know is that Milo is standing in front of me, and I can hardly control how much I want him to be closer.

I lean in, pausing a moment before our lips touch to ask for permission. He meets me, and my world suddenly spins out. There's something different in this kiss, something hungry.

When I feel my back press into the countertop, a small noise escapes me. This time, I don't pull away.

"Shh," Milo whispers, running his lips gently along my neck. It sends shivers over my entire body. "You have to be quiet."

"I am being quiet," I hiss.

A breathy laugh leaves those lips that are lighting my flesh on fire. "Are you saying I should make it more challenging?" he asks, and I fight to catch my breath. There isn't anything I want more.

"Sure," I whisper. "I'm up for the challenge." I have no idea what has gotten into me, but now I'm taunting him and pressing closer while holding onto the countertop for dear life.

Milo nips at the skin just beneath my ear, his hand coming up under my tank top to run along my torso. It isn't until I feel his hands moving lower that I catch his full meaning.

I let out a quick breath, and he pulls away. "Is this okay?" he asks. With that one question, my heart pounds even faster, and I know I have full control over what happens next. Something about having that kind of control drives me forward.

I nod before pressing my lips to his again.

When I feel his fingertips trace over the waistline of my shorts, a spark of anticipation lights up my chest.

I make a small noise, and Milo lets out a breathy chuckle. "Looks like I'm winning," he taunts.

"Absolutely not," I retort.

It only takes a second before his finger dips below my waistband and he's there, sending ripples of pleasure through my body.

"The last time I was here," he says between kisses. "It was purely professional."

"I know," I confirm, recalling one of the most embarrassing moments of my life.

His eyes darken as he looks down at me, his hand stilling right where I need him. "This time," he says. "It is absolutely *not* professional, Olive."

That's when Dr. Jameson shows me exactly what he means.

TWENTY-TWO

Since moving to Minnesota for school, I've become accustomed to flying on airplanes even though it isn't my favorite activity. The plane is always loud, and boring, and mostly loud. Something about the constant air blowing into the cabin annoys me and I usually put in headphones and pretend I'm at one of the concerts I love so much.

On the flight back, I don't do that though. Milo is sitting next to me looking through whatever pamphlet they placed in the seatback in front of him when the plane finally starts moving for takeoff.

The flight attendants go through their typical presentation of how to buckle your seatbelt and when to put your oxygen mask on should the cabin's air pressure change.

It's all incredibly droll.

"You never answered my question last night," I point out while fiddling with the small piece of plastic that holds my tray in place. I can't release it now, since we are roaming around the asphalt waiting for takeoff, but then I'm nervous about what I'm saying. I need something to keep myself busy to avoid the fear of what Milo's answer may be.

Especially after last night.

Milo licks his bottom lip, and I can't help thinking about how it felt on my skin last night. "Are you asking me to be your boyfriend, Olive?"

I huff a laugh. "Why does that sound juvenile?" I ask, avoiding the question because I'm still terrified.

"Your partner," he supplies. His hand reaches up to still my own, bringing it down to the armrest between us and weaving his fingers through mine. "I'll be whatever you want me to be. I think I've earned a title after cleaning vomit from the carpet of your childhood home."

I snort at that, relief washing over me as I rest my head on the chair-back. Milo's hand is warm, and I'm suddenly thinking about where it was again. I can feel my face heat at the thought.

"Are you okay?" he asks, genuine concern in his tone.

No, I'm thinking about how absolutely not professional you were and how I want to do that again.

"I'm fine. I was just thinking."

"Did you—" he pauses nervously. "Did you want that to be my answer?"

My head snaps in his direction. "Yes!" My brows furrow. "Of course."

"Okay, good."

We both settle in as the flight takes off, listening to the sounds of people snoring and murmuring on the plane. About twenty minutes in, I realize I need to use the restroom.

Milo graciously gets up and helps me into the aisle so I can take care of my practically overflowing bladder. He doesn't make comments about the concert of the loading dock, but I definitely think of that memory fondly. Thank all the gods I don't have to pee *that* badly.

When I walk out of the restroom, my eye catches on familiar faces conversing toward the front of the plane just beyond where Milo is sitting.

I leap into the seat next to Milo, barely able to contain myself.

"Milo, Cerebellum is on the flight!"

His brows furrow. "Like the part of the brain?"

"No, the band!" I'm whisper yelling as I gesture ahead of us, causing Milo to peek his head out into the aisle.

"A band you like?" He asks.

"Curly Fries opened up for them a long time ago. I've talked to the band members before, since I've been following them forever." I keep stealing glances in their direction, trying to not be noticed. "I don't think they want to be bothered, though, but isn't it crazy to have the entire band on the flight?"

"There's a band on the flight?" The flight attendant is smiling down at us, her sharp nose raised slightly. "Do you want me to say something?" she asks.

"No!" I shoot back. Lord, if she says something to Cerebellum, I'm going to look like the craziest, most annoying fan to ever exist.

"Not a problem, drinks?"

When the flight attendant walks away from us, Milo leans in to whisper, "I don't think she's going to listen to your request at keeping silent about the band."

"What makes you say that?" I ask.

He points up to where the woman is standing next to the phone on the plane.

When she starts talking, I try to melt away in my seat. Milo is laughing, which at this point is kind of offensive. I just want it all to stop.

"I've been informed by the birthday girl that there's a band on our flight today." People start looking around the plane, and I can almost feel the collective groan from every guy in Cerebellum.

"This is my fault," I whisper.

"No," Milo consoles. "It's actually hers. I also didn't know it was your birthday." The mocking in his tone has frustration bubbling up in my chest.

"It's not," I hiss.

The flight attendant keeps talking. "Why don't you guys sing a song for us?"

Why is my life like this?

"No, that's fine!" Milo shouts, desperately trying to ease the pain I'm currently feeling.

The band, of course, declines, but I see the way Jesse catches sight of me. I know he recognizes me because I've been to so many shows.

He also gave me the setlist earlier this year before I found out he had a girlfriend.

This could not be worse.

I try to keep my head down and stay quiet through the rest of the flight.

In an attempt to change the subject, Milo takes a sip of water from the plane before talking. "I had fun meeting your family. You should come to Colorado sometime."

I look up at him, my heart warming at the request. "That would be nice."

~

Milo: I want to see you tomorrow.

I roll over in my bed back at my apartment and bite my lip while staring at my phone.

Milo dropped me off here a few hours ago, and he has to work on Saturdays since the clinic is open.

Me: What time do you work until?

Milo: Eight.

I don't mind being out late since it's the weekend, and classes don't resume until Wednesday. I also don't understand if his response is an offer to see me, or he's trying to say he can't actually do anything.

Me: Oh.

The next message has my stomach flipping. The notification shines on my device.

Milo: I'm dying without you, here.

An idea for a text comes to my mind, but I have to muster up the courage to say it. I decide to type the message, anyway.

Me: We wouldn't want you to die. There were so many useful things you showed me just recently. It would be awful if you couldn't do that anymore.

Milo: Olive Finch, are you the one sending spicy messages now?

Me: Maybe.

Milo: Maybe next time I can show you more.

Tons of images flash through my mind with those eight words and I sincerely hope he's wanting me to see him tomorrow.

Me: I don't think I would mind that.

TWENTY-THREE

Milo was serious, and now I'm standing in the office of the Urgent Care I visited earlier this year. When the woman at the desk calls me forward, I recognize her red hair and the smattering of freckles across her face instantly.

My memory betrays me, and I cringe as the image of me explaining why I was here plays through my mind like an old film.

"Can I help you?" she says sweetly, without looking up from her computer.

"Um, yes." I'm fidgeting with my coral-colored turtleneck, desperate to keep my voice steady. "I'm actually here to see Milo." She looks up at me. "Dr. Jameson, I mean."

"Do you have an appointment?" she asks. When her green eyes meet mine, something sparks there. "You've been here before," she remarks.

I slouch, trying to make myself seem smaller. "Yeah, I have." I clear my throat.

"So, Dr. Jameson—"

"Is expecting you," she finishes. "Dr. McMillian is done for the night. He can walk you back to the office."

Great. Dr. Scowls-a-lot.

Sitting in the waiting room, I can hardly keep my knees from bouncing up and down. My eyes skim over the gray walls and bland décor that you would expect of a doctor's office. The room is sterile, and I suppose that's all you can ask for.

"Olive," the old man grunts when the door opens. I stand up quickly, grabbing my small purse and strapping it across my torso.

Dr. McMillian is even grumpier than I remember. His gray hair is cut short, and he walks slowly as he leads me to the back.

We pass the different patient rooms until we come to a room at the back, complete with a desk and chair.

"You can wait here," Dr. McMillian huffs, closing the door and exiting promptly.

My eyes catch to the photographs on Milo's desk. There's a picture of Milo with what I believe to be his parents. Milo is holding up a small fluffy dog and flashing his winning smile.

I trail my fingers over the photograph before sitting down in his chair. I spin once before noticing the silver mini-refrigerator beneath his desk. There are word magnets littering the front of it in no particular order.

Tapping my fingers on the desk, I decide to busy myself since it isn't quite eight yet. Milo should be done in the next five minutes.

I draft the best poem I have ever crafted, looking at my finished work.

Eat Good Water Wet Turtle.

Man Eat.

He Balloon Ball Fat.

I laugh and admire my handiwork when the door clicks open. Glancing at the clock, I realize it's ten minutes past eight.

Milo's presence startles me, and I jump back a bit.

"Sorry about being late. Things sometimes run over with patients." He halts, his gaze flicking to the fridge beneath his desk. "What are you working on?"

"I believe," I say, spinning his chair from side to side. "That you are looking at the next Hemmingway."

Milo chuckles and walks over to admire my work. He kneels down to get a closer look. I notice that he's wearing a pair of black slacks and a button-up that tugs tightly at his chest. The rolled-up sleeves have my heart picking up in pace.

"Wow," he muses, turning to look up at me as I sit in his chair. "You've crafted something truly beautiful. Everyone who enters my office is going to be asking who the poet is." He stands up and offers me his hand, which I take easily. "Too bad I'm a man, and I will absolutely take full credit for the work you put in."

I scoff, holding back a smile. "You're truly like all the rest of them."

"Awe, that's not true," he says, while pulling me closer. His arms wrap around my waist, and he peers down at me. "For starters, I am an above-average painter." He nods toward the window, and I look over to see a selfie of the two of us with our painted pumpkins held up from our first date. My heart warms.

"I added that today," he said. "I've had it printed, but now that you're my girlfriend, partner, whatever-you-want-to-call-it, I decided you deserved a spot in my office."

"I'm glad you didn't shove me in the corner." I look up at him and smile, resting one of my hands on his chest. "It's much nicer by the window. At least there, it doesn't feel like I'm a prisoner."

"You think being with me means you're a prisoner?" he scowls.

"Absolutely not." I stand on my toes, planting a soft kiss on his lips. "Stop scowling," I scold. "You look like your mentor."

Milo laughs and pulls away, grabbing a backpack from behind his desk.

"Let's get out of here," he says, lacing his fingers through mine and dragging me to the door.

~

Milo's house is just as I remembered it, the scent of vanilla and cashmere invading my senses as I sit on the couch.

"What do you want to watch?" he asks, bringing in a bowl of popcorn.

The entire scene is familiar as he flips on the television and winds his arm around me, tucking me closer.

"You choose," I say. "I chose last time."

Milo smiles and flips through the choices. When he clicks on *Mamma Mia! Here We Go Again*, I can't help the smile that pulls at my lips.

"Good choice," I comment.

"I thought so."

We settle in as the movie starts. While it plays, Milo is laughing and making comments. He's engaging in the entire thing and remembers the plot of the first one.

"How do you remember these?" I finally ask.

Milo runs a hand down his face. "I've been caught," he says, his cheeks pink. "My sister loves them."

I gently smack him on the chest. "You liar!" I accuse. "This whole time I thought you were watching these for me, and you just liked me so much you wanted to learn everything about the movies I like."

An unfamiliar look crosses his face after what I said. It's soft, and there's something there I can't quite read. Milo pushes back my hair, glancing down at my lips briefly before his gaze meets my eyes again. "I do like you, Olive," he whispers. "I like you a lot."

Tension crackles, but I'm distracted by the urgent call my bladder is making to my brain. I place a quick kiss on his lips before standing up.

"Where's your bathroom?" I ask.

Milo sits forward, resting his elbows on his knees. He points casually with one hand toward the kitchen. "Through the kitchen, down the hall, and to the right."

His cheeks are still tinted when I nod and walk away, leaving to find the restroom and relieve myself.

Milo's bathroom is painted a dark shade of green with sleek black tile, and a clean sink. I wash my hands after using the toilet and walk out into the hall.

Just across from the restroom is a wooden door that is cracked. Inside, I can see a full-sized bed with a black comforter and accent pillows.

"Well, we love that," I mutter, pushing the door gently with my hand. It creaks a little, and I look over my shoulder to ensure that I'm still alone.

Milo's bedroom is simple and clean. I walk in, running my finger along the large wooden dresser just across from the bed.

"Finding everything you need?"

I startle at the sound of Milo's voice from the doorway.

When I turn, he's leaning against the entrance to the bedroom, his arms folded across his broad chest.

"I got curious," I admit.

Something darkens in his eyes. "About my bedroom?" he asks, raising a brow.

I swallow hard. How he's looking at me sends fire skittering along my skin. Every nerve is lighted with sensation, and I'm now struggling to keep my breath down.

"I guess." I try to keep my tone steady, but it still comes out a little breathless.

Milo pushes off the wall and walks toward me. His hand cups the side of my face and he runs the pad of his thumb over my cheek, trailing it down until it ghosts over my bottom lip, catching just slightly before it rests on my jawline.

"What did you want to know about my bedroom, exactly?" Milo's voice is low, and I can feel my stomach curling and the fire growing hotter on my skin. It feels like my flesh is on fire.

I'm not sure how I should respond. My mind is going a thousand miles an hour trying to figure out what I should do.

I think back to the text where he had said he wanted to show me more, and there's a part of me that wants to know what he meant by it.

And when I say a part of me, I don't mean half; I mean like a giant chunk.

Milo leans forward slowly, and his lips brush over mine with the gentlest pressure. "Hmm?" he muses before nipping at my bottom lip. I gasp at the gesture.

"I just thought I could learn something," Words are hard with him crowding my senses like this.

Milo's chuckle and dark and rumbles through his chest. "I think I might be able to show you something," he says.

My voice is barely a whisper. "Okay."

Milo's lips are on mine, and his hands are running down my neck, over my shoulders, my arms, and my waist. I can't think past the touch that is burning through my clothes—can't think past the smell of vanilla and popcorn filling the room.

I don't really know what to do, but when I bite his bottom lip gently, he hisses out a breath, and something about that has me wanting to do it again. I would do anything to hear him make that sound.

Milo's hand tugs on the front of my sweater, pulling it free from my jeans. His skin is warm when it touches the flesh of my stomach. He pauses before moving any higher.

"This is still okay, right?" he asks, and I practically melt.

"Yes," I whisper.

The lights are dim in his room, and his hand is skating higher until he's running his thumb over my breast, sending shivers down my spine.

When Milo leans forward, I back up until my legs hit the bed, sending me sitting on the edge.

"You have a lot of accent pillows for a man," I jest, trying my best to keep myself from ripping the buttons on his shirt off the fabric.

Milo chuckles, tugging my sweater over my head between kisses. "Don't mock me for having my life together," he defends.

"I wasn't." Milo is unbuttoning his shirt in front of me, and I swallow, my mind becoming a lust-filled haze.

"I have so many pillows for a reason," he says, smiling.

My brows crease in confusion. Milo peels off his shirt. "They're good for offering some extra support—a decent angle."

My cheeks flush. "I don't catch your meaning."

Milo leans over me, slowly unbuttoning his pants as I lie back on the bed, scooting back toward the plethora of cushions.

"If you're still okay," he says, leaning down to kiss my neck. "I'd like to show you."

TWENTY-FOUR

Sometime between Thanksgiving and the week before Christmas, I realized that I hardly spent any time at my apartment at all.

Milo had stayed over a few times, but Jafar had his own food bowl and is currently curled up next to me while I sit on the couch sipping decaffeinated chai and Facetiming Jo.

"I think I'm going to quit my job," she says, holding the phone so I can see Elias in the shot.

"Do it. That place is toxic," I respond. Elias is jumping over his toys and pretending to be a superhero.

I hear the front door open and set down my mug. "Hey, I have to go. Milo's back."

"Tell him I said hi!" she says. "Make sure he's treating you right and tell him he should try—"

I hang up the phone before she can get another word in. It was probably inappropriate anyway.

"Hey," he says, taking off his coat. His cheeks are red from the cold winter air outside. "I have good news and bad news."

"Bad news first," I say, trying to hide the way nerves start taking over my body.

"I have to work on Christmas."

I frown. Milo had considered coming home with me in just over a week before Christmas. I was looking forward to having him come home with me and get to know my family more. I still hadn't met his parents, but I did FaceTime once with them last week. He wanted to take me there after the new year.

"Okay, and the good news?"

Milo plops on the couch next to me, suddenly smiling. "I got tomorrow off for your birthday."

"What?" I turn toward him, propping one leg up on the couch. Jafar jumps onto the coffee table, and I shoo him down before he can lick my tea. "You did?"

"I drive a hard bargain," he says. "If they wouldn't let me take the twenty-fifth, they had to let me take the fourteenth."

I slouch back on the couch. I can't help but smile. Tiffany flew out to visit one of her friends, so I thought I was going to be spending my birthday alone with Jafar. "Am I allowed to know what the plan is?"

Milo reaches in his pocket, and I can tell by his face that he has some grand thing planned for my birthday. He pulls out what looks like two concert tickets, and I sit up abruptly, snatching them from his hands.

"Cerebellum!" I screech. Something about how thoughtful the date is makes my heart sing. I didn't even realize they were playing a show in town.

Milo kisses my temple and takes the tickets back for safekeeping. "I thought you'd want to go." I can tell he's proud of his surprise. The fact of the matter is, he deserves to be proud. It was a really good move. "I only have one request before we go," he says.

"Literally anything." My body is too excited to question what his request may be.

"You have to use the restroom before we show up."

I laugh, leaning back on the couch and smiling up at the ceiling. If Milo can't go home with me for Christmas, this is the next best thing.

"You, my good sir, have a deal."

~

"Do you think they're going to remember you from the plane?" Milo asks as he nudges my shoulder.

I look up to the stage, awaiting Cerebellum to come out onto the stage after the opener.

"God, I hope not."

It doesn't take long for the crowd to start screaming as the stage fills up with members of the band. Milo and I join them, excited for the show.

As the first song begins to play, I can feel every strum of the guitar or the beat of the drum running through my blood. It's a reminder of why I love these concerts. There's something freeing about joining a group of people and screaming your favorite music without a care.

I've played enough of their songs around Milo that he knows every word and shouts each single one into the crowd.

This morning, he had surprised me by making breakfast and taking care of Jafar's first and second breakfast.

Honestly, that cat is becoming too spoiled around my boyfriend.

Somewhere close to the end of the set, I look over into the crowd and my eyes catch on a familiar face. Dread fills my core as I look to see Margot glaring daggers at me.

Milo notices and looks her direction as well.

"Who's that?" he asks above the sound of the music.

The lights are flashing overhead, and everyone is jumping with the song. My mood is utterly foul. "My old roommate," I confess. "She's kind of a bitch."

"Then I don't like her."

Margot pushes her way through the crowd. When she gets close to us, she plasters on a fake smile while holding an open cup of beer.

"Olive!" she shouts. "It's so good to see you. Is this the guy you went out with a few months ago? I thought you said he was just a guy you went on a few dates with."

My blood boils. She's intentionally trying to get me to feel uncomfortable, which is typical for her. I can feel the rage thrashing in my chest like a caged animal ready to break free. I ignore her comment.

"This is Dr. Milo Jameson," I say over the music. "He's my boyfriend."

"Awe," she squeals, but the sound isn't genuine. "That's so sweet!" Margot tucks a strand of hair behind her ear. "I didn't think it was anything serious by the way you were talking. Hi, Milo. I'm Margot."

Margot holds her hand out, and Milo respectfully shakes it. She slithers in close like a snake and continues talking, blocking me out of the conversation. "So," she begins. "You're a doctor. I bet you see all sorts of crazy things at work!"

"Sometimes." Milo's thin smile shows me he's completely disinterested in starting up a conversation with my trashy ex-roommate.

"Well, maybe you can take a break from Olive and check me out sometime."

That harlot!

The caged beast that was desperate to release its wrath on the woman in front of me pounds on the bars. There's nothing else I can do but let it out.

Without thinking, I take the drink in my hand and dump it out on Margot, my face twisted in disgust.

She doesn't waste time throwing her drink at me, and before I can reach forward to claw her beady eyes out, Milo is dragging me away from the stage and toward the quiet hallway by the bathroom.

When I finally get settled on a bench in the hall, Milo brings damp napkins and starts wiping the beer from my face and clothes while kneeling in front of me.

"My sweet Olive has thorns," he says, gently sliding the napkin over my cheek.

I can't help but laugh. Now that the anger has dissipated, I see the situation for what it really was.

When the laughter subsides, I look at Milo in front of me. There's no judgment on his face. "That felt so good." I'm smiling brightly and taking a napkin from his hand to scrub at my sweater.

"I like this villainous side of you," Milo says, his voice dropping lower as he leans in. "It's getting me all worked up."

Heat instantly rises to my cheeks, lighting that familiar fire.

"We could leave the concert and go back to your house," I suggest, raising a brow. "I'm sure Jafar misses you."

Milo licks his lips, skimming a hand up the outside of my thigh before standing up. When he reaches his hand out to help me off the bench, he smiles.

"Absolutely."

TWENTY-FIVE

I didn't realize how difficult Christmas would be without Milo. Going home to Indiana was nice, and I was thankful to see my parents, but there was a sense of sorrow wrapped around the holiday—choking out joy like thick vines winding up the trunk of a tree.

Back in Minnesota, I'm hundreds of miles away from life's problems, but then returning has guilt pounding in my chest like I've done some kind of grand injustice by not being here.

My grandfather declined steadily, which at eighty-seven years old, it isn't necessarily a surprise. He's in a wheelchair now, wrapped in blankets while my family gathers around the Christmas tree, opening gifts.

The only thing that keeps my heart from cracking painfully is the contented look on his face as he watches Elias open a set of dinosaur action figures. The way my nephew squeals with excitement has my grandfather laughing, my grandmother patting him on the leg as he does. There is sorrow there too. It's like everyone knows he is dying, but nobody will say anything.

I haven't had a lot of experiences with death. My cousin, Jo, had two friends pass away in high school. I only had to walk through the death of our dogs, and while that kind of death brings on a sting of its own, it is nothing compared to this.

Me: Wish you were here.

I'm hoping Milo responds, but he's been busy all day.

"Olive, it looks like there are more gifts over here for you." My aunt, Laura, passes a gift across the mounting pile of discarded wrapping paper.

I tear the paper away and uncap the box to reveal a new t-shirt that my grandmother bought. "Thanks, Grammie," I say, offering a wane smile.

Milo still hasn't texted, and the sadness becomes a deep well within my heart—a well that is practically overflowing with emotion.

"Excuse me," I say, walking to the restroom. When I call Milo while sitting on the toilet, wiping my tears with my sleeve, the disappointment becomes a tangible object. The ringing turns to his voicemail, and I don't bother leaving a message.

I put my phone on airplane mode, touch up my makeup in the mirror above the sink, and muster up the courage to enjoy one last Christmas to the man who played such an important role in my life.

He was the one everyone went to when the world was falling apart—the anchor in the storm. It's hard to believe that our time with him is limited, but I'll be damned if I don't make the best of it.

~

Sitting in my bed at home, my phone goes off. I fly back tomorrow, and I'm looking forward to spending time with Milo. Jafar is curled up next to me on top of the blankets, and I know he's going to absolutely kill me when I put him back in the cat carrier for the flight.

Milo: My friends are having a New Year's Eve party, and I want you to come with me. Lillian and Juliette will be there.

The prospect of meeting the rest of Milo's friends should excite me, but something about the text unsettles me. I haven't been in the headspace for fun activities lately.

Milo has been extremely busy all week, and I've descended into a level of sadness that I haven't struggled with since my sophomore year of college. I know my mom probably has my old anti-depressants somewhere upstairs, but I can't bring myself to go back to that place, even if they aren't expired yet.

I had been doing really well. I don't like the feeling that one sad event in my life could lead me to feeling that level of numbness and loneliness again. I refuse to accept it.

Me: That would be great! I can't wait to see you tomorrow.

It takes a while for the text to come through, and I sigh, rolling out of bed to go upstairs and get something to eat.

Milo: I miss you, Olive. I'm sorry I've been so busy.

His apology is completely unnecessary, but it settles something inside me. I smile as I walk up the stairs, thankful that I will get to return to some normalcy.

Going back to Minnesota seems a little like running away from the problem, and I feel guilty about that. Maybe I shouldn't.

I feel like a mess, and I'm not sure I'm going to get out of this funk anytime soon.

My mom is standing in the kitchen when I walk inside. I feel like a child again, standing in my socks, shorts, and a t-shirt, asking about food.

When she looks at me, my face twists and my eyes sting.

"Oh honey," she says, walking forward and embracing me.

Somewhere in the warmth of her hug, I find it in me to allow all the emotion to spill out. The sobs wrack my body, and she strokes my hair gently.

"What is this about?" she asks, but I think she knows.

"BopBop is dying," I say, and I see the tears gather at the corners of her own eyes, and I feel stupid for being so self-centered. As if she doesn't feel the same heavy sorrow I'm feeling. He's her father.

She pulls me in tighter and my tears run free, staining her shirt.

"BopBop is dying. I'm going to be stuck hundreds of miles away when it happens."

"That's not true, honey." My mother says. There's a strength in her voice as she speaks. "We will get you home if that's what you want, Olive. You're not alone."

It's in that moment I let myself break apart.

TWENTY-SIX

Snow is falling in thick flakes when I walk to Regulation Red on the morning of New Year's Eve. Milo is supposed to pick me up around eight, but he has to spend the first half of the day at the office. At first, I didn't mind only seeing him Sundays and the occasional evenings, but after my trip home, the time he has to spend at work for his residency is really getting to me.

I keep reminding myself that I shouldn't be selfish, though.

"Can I get the chai hot this morning?" I ask Ezra, trying to plaster a smile on my face.

"Anything for you, Olive." Ezra types in my order behind the counter, and the familiarity of the situation brings me some peace. "How are things going with the doctor?" he asks.

"Fantastic." I hand him my card, and as I really think on it, things with Milo *are* good. I couldn't ask for someone who treats me better. I'm just feeling alone right now, but it's my own emotions messing with me. He hasn't actually done anything wrong. In fact, he spent half of the morning texting me spicy messages.

My cheeks heat at the thought. "How is your love life?" I ask, trying to move my thoughts away from those messages. "It seems like you're always asking about mine. Still single?"

"Uh—" Ezra rubs the back of his neck nervously, and I swear I see a blush on his face. Something about it brings me joy—real joy. "Actually no. I'm seeing someone."

"Sounds promising," I say, walking to the pickup counter. There's nobody in line, so he moves over, resting his elbows on the counter's surface.

"It is. I'm actually really excited about it."

"Do you give her free oat milk, too?" I ask, allowing the smile to lift my lips.

"Only for you, Olive." Ezra winks, and I grab my Chai off the counter.

~

Milo texted me and ended up back at my apartment early to hang out since the doctor's office was slow. With everywhere my mind has been lately, I was thankful for the company.

Jafar is chasing the toy that I'm dangling in front of him and then moving swiftly across the floor. I laugh when he misses, but at one point, his claw catches my hand, and I wince, sucking the wound to keep it from stinging.

"Ouch, you asshole!"

"Didn't you listen to my presentation during Thanksgiving?" Milo strides out of the bathroom wearing black pants, a sweater, and a beanie—already shedding the outfit from work.

"I listened to it!" I defend. "That doesn't mean I agree with it! The cat is a monster."

Milo sits in front of me, and that stupid monster curls up in his lap and immediately starts purring. My glare could shoot shards of ice at them both.

"He's misunderstood," Milo says, scratching him behind the ears. "Aren't you, buddy?"

I scoff, throwing the toy across the room into the appropriate box without getting up.

"Okay," Milo begins, his face turning serious. "What's wrong?"

"What? Nothing." I don't understand what he's talking about. I'm just sitting on the floor in his oversized t-shirt, waiting until it's time to get ready for the party.

"You've been off since Christmas. Is it something I did?"

I suddenly feel bad about how distant I've been. I cringe. "No, it's not about you. I've just been—" I fight for the right word, my brow creasing. "Sad."

"Your grandfather?" he asks.

"He's dying," I say, hoping that the more I say it, the less it will sting when it happens. I groan and lie back on the floor, staring at my ceiling. The fan spins, and I try to lock my gaze on one blade and follow it around the room. "I'm so far away, I won't be there to help. I know my mom is stressed. I just feel so selfish. It feels like I'm running away and living in my own perfect bubble here with you."

I turn to look at Milo as he gingerly moves Jafar from his lap. He lies on the floor next to me, threading his fingers through mine. There's a comfort in his presence, and it eases the ache in my chest.

"You're not being selfish, Olive," he says. "Just because life brings sorrow doesn't mean you have to force yourself to feel it always. It doesn't make you a bad person to behold the beauty of stars during the darkest of nights."

"Wow," I remark, brows lifted. "Forget my poem at your office. You really are the talented one."

Milo lets out a breathy chuckle. He lifts our hands above our heads, taking his other hand and tracing my fingers with it. "All I'm saying is you don't have to punish yourself for experiencing happiness. It doesn't make you a bad granddaughter. Sadness and joy can exist together. Not everything is black and white."

I smile at him, running my gaze over his full lips, and the way his stubble is already peeking through on his jawline. I lean over quickly, stealing a kiss from his cheek.

Milo leans over, pinning me down to the floor, and I shriek, sending Jafar sprinting into the bedroom.

"You're a thief, Olive Finch."

"I swear on everything I am. If you say I've stolen your heart, I will vomit. That will immediately give me the ick. You cannot say it." I gaze up at him, and he's wearing a smirk.

"Good thing I wasn't going to say that," he comments, his eyes lighted.

"What were you going to say, then?"

Milo plants a kiss on my lips before pulling away. "You're wearing my shirt, you buffoon." Milo stands up and offers me his hand. I take it and get up as well.

"Right," I say, looking down. I tug at the hem of the shirt. Since Milo is tall, it falls mid-thigh on me. "I should probably get changed, anyway. We have to go soon."

Milo nudges me with his shoulder. "Exactly." He smiles, and I can't help the way my nerves light up at his expression and the way he's standing so close to me. "Would you hate me if I admitted you stole the other thing, too?"

Confusion takes over my expression before I register his meaning. I swat at his chest playfully. "Absolutely. If you say it, we're going to have issues."

"Wouldn't want to upset the boss," he jokes, holding up his hands defensively.

I walk off down the hallway, trying to think about what I will wear for the party tonight.

"You're wrong," I shout from my bedroom.

"About what?" he hollers back.

I laugh as I pick out a shirt from my closet. "Jafar is the boss!"

TWENTY-SEVEN

Glitter and black and gold streamers that descended from the high ceilings decorated the pottery studio. I wasn't expecting such a large amount of people, but Milo convinced me to invite Tiffany, so I was thankful there would be someone here that I knew.

I don't think I could bear meeting new people all night.

Milo squeezes my hand three times before opening the glass door into the studio. The scent of champagne and the sound of music coming from speakers on the far wall greet us.

"Why do you seem so nervous?" Milo asks, leaning into me slightly. I look down at my boots, unable to hide the truth there.

I chose a black velvet baby doll top, jeans, and my boots. Milo said the other people in attendance wouldn't dress up, and that brought me some comfort.

"I don't know," I respond. "Something about being around all of your friends makes me nervous." My eyes meet his. "They're all older than me. I haven't met anyone aside from Lillian. I just—"

Milo releases my hand and drags me against his side by putting his arm around my shoulders. He kisses my temple. "So, you're worried because you feel like I haven't showed you off?" His thumb brushes against my shoulder. "One, I work a lot, so this *is* my chance to show you off, and two, who cares if they're older than you? It doesn't make a difference to me."

I smile at that just as Lillian strides over. She's wearing a shimmering gold bodysuit and black jeans, her face bright when she sees us.

"Olive!" she says, dragging me in for a hug. "It's so good to see you again. I hope you loved your mug."

"It's a little lopsided, but I had fun making it."

Lillian gives me a sly look. "I'm sure you did." She winks.

Milo grabs my hand again. "Where's Juliette?"

Lillian looks around, her dark braids hanging down to her waist at her back. "She's around here somewhere." Milo told me more about Juliette and Lillian and how they ended up together. From everything I've heard, they have the type of relationship people dream of. When Juliette realized she no longer wanted to be a doctor and wanted to pursue art, Lillian was the one who encouraged her where so many people believed she was throwing her life away. "There!" Lillian points, and I follow to where a tall woman with a lean figure is pointing out a table of cupcakes to guests.

"Oh lord," Lillian groans. "She made those cupcakes last night. They're champagne cupcakes—full of booze. Tread lightly or you'll lose your cute outfit." Lillian pats my arm and walks over to her wife to point us out.

Juliette strides over, her black hair piled into a messy bun atop her head. It somehow looks as though every strand of hair is placed perfectly. "Is this her?" she asks Milo.

"In the flesh." The pride in his done stirs something in me, releasing my fears from earlier.

"Olive!" she says, going in for a hug. She pauses before embracing me. "Can I hug you?" I laugh and nod, even though I still find hugs between strangers to be awkward.

What if she can tell everything about my soul from this one hug, and she determines I'm not good enough?

When she pulls away, she immediately starts talking. "I'm sorry I didn't get to meet you the day you guys were here! Milo talks about you constantly. I'm just so happy he's found someone to deal with his shit." Her head glances back at the dessert table briefly. "You need to try these cupcakes!" She's suddenly dragging me across the floor, weaving between people. Juliette looks over her shoulder. "I made them last night." Her voice drops to a whisper as she leans in. "They're filled with alcohol."

I laugh as I glance back at Milo, who is now standing and talking with Lillian. I mouth the words *help me*, to which Milo responds with a chuckle and a mouthed *no* in response.

~

Me: Where are you?

Tiffany: I'm on my way, I swear! I just had to pick something up first.

I slide my phone in my back pocket, looking back toward the giant *Jenga* game they have set up. I'm currently winning against Lillian in the tournament we started. The game makes me miss Elias. Last summer, we played at a graduation party together. It mostly consisted of him removing and replacing the same block and then getting overly excited when he accidentally tipped the tower. But it doesn't change my feelings.

I hear the bell chime over the music and look over to see Tiffany walking in with Corrine just behind her.

"Oh, my god!" I yell, running to my friends to greet them. "What are you doing here?" I ask Corrine.

"I was trying to keep it a surprise," she replies. "I also wanted to meet the doctor."

As if on cue, Milo appears beside me with a hard seltzer drink that he places in my hand.

"Do you guys need drinks?" he asks, ready to turn around and get them whatever they need.

"Yes!" Corrine says. "I had a late flight, and I'm dying to test out the karaoke machine in the corner."

She's gone before I can say another word.

"Are we going to be doing karaoke?" Milo asks me. He doesn't seem opposed to the idea.

"Only if you promise to sing very, very badly." I press the can to my lips and take a drink.

Milo leans in, and I can feel his breath ghost over the flesh beneath my ear. "Can't promise that," he says. "I'm just as fantastic at singing as I am at painting."

I snort. "Then you're going to fulfill the promise whether you like it or not. That portrait was terrible."

"Well, don't get me started on your poetry." He wraps an arm around my shoulders and drags me to his chest.

I look up at him, barely able to keep my voice from sounding offended. I know he doesn't believe me though, because I'm grinning as I speak. "That poem was a masterpiece! The juxtaposition between the turtle and the eating man—"

"You're not using the word juxtaposition right."

I raise a brow at him. "Don't you dare try to mansplain when I'm just bullshitting."

"Fine, fine. You're a poet, and Corrine is a professional vocalist. She's already picking up the microphone."

I drag Milo over to the karaoke machine, and for the first time since before Christmas, I realize I'm actually having fun.

~

When the countdown begins, the entire studio is humming with excited energy. Juliette got a large television working and has it stationed on the desk at the front of the room. Everyone is holding drinks and yelling while the streamers glitter in the dim lights.

When I look up at Milo, he looks completely content, and I have to admit that meeting his friends warms something in me. Milo places his hand on my cheek as everyone shouts around us. His breath is warm as it ghosts against my skin, and I can smell the alcohol on his breath mixed with the vanilla scent that reminds me of *him*.

"I really like you, Olive."

I bite my lip, butterflies dancing in my stomach. "I really like you too."

"Even though I'm a terrible painter, a worse singer, and spend most of my days looking at the boobs of old women in my office?" The humorous smirk on his face has my cheeks heating, and I place my hand on his chest.

"Even then, Dr. Jameson."

Milo leans down as the countdown rounds out, everyone shouting as we bring in the new year. The room is a cacophony of cheers and noisemakers while Milo's mouth hovers over mine, waiting to kiss me.

"Happy New Year, Olive Finch."

"Happy New Year."

TWENTY-EIGHT

Something woke me up in the middle of the night. I grab my phone to check for any messages, but there's nothing there. Just the time—two in the morning.

I rub my eyes and roll over, desperately trying to go back to sleep. New Year's was absolutely perfect a few nights ago, and I think of Corrine screaming a Cerebellum song into the karaoke microphone with me. We were pretty drunk by that time, and Cerebellum wasn't even an option, so we chose a random song and sang the lyrics, anyway. I laugh and try to close my eyes.

It isn't long before I feel my phone vibrating on my bed. Jafar quickly jumps down from the mattress and skitters off down the hall. He hates the vibrations from my phone and usually retreats when he's subject to its assault.

I see my mom's number light up on the phone, and something inside of me just *knows*.

I feel nothing when I answer.

"Hello?"

"Liv?" My mom sounds like she's been crying. "Aunt Laura and Aunt Valarie are here." There's a pause, and I can hear someone murmur in the background. I sit up, wiping the sleep from my eyes.

Jafar comes back in, jumping and placing himself on my lap while I flip on the lamp.

"It's BopBop."

My entire world stops.

I don't cry, or wail, or even move a muscle. It's as if the entire world has gone dark and silent, and I'm fighting to hear my mother on the line. Reality hasn't set in, and I run my shaking fingers over Jafar's fur, desperate to seek comfort somewhere for the moment when my emotions blow apart.

"I need to go," my mother says, and I barely register her words. "I'm booking your flight now, but we are driving to Grammie's. I love you, Liv. I'll call you when we figure out what's going on."

"Is he dead?" I croak, not wanting to hear the words. My mind is like a broken record, playing my thoughts on repeat.

You weren't there. You were at a party with Milo. You weren't there. You weren't there. Everyone was there but you. You were hundreds of miles away and consumed with your own life. You weren't there.

"Yes, honey. He passed in his sleep. I'll call you later."

The phone disconnects, and I'm left in my dim room alone and surrounded by darkness.

It washes over me slowly, and I can't help the rising sorrow or panic that fills my chest. I'm suddenly taken back to the hallway with Milo on Thanksgiving, and desperately wanting that kind of comfort. My mother is busy trying to figure everything out. I can't ask her to comfort me right now.

As the tears flow, slowly turning to sobs, I send a text message to Milo through blurry eyesight. It's so late, but I don't care.

Me: He's gone. I need someone.

Me: I wasn't there, Milo.

Me: I wasn't there.

There's no response, so I get myself out of bed and move to the kitchen. I try calling Tiffany, then Corrine, but Corrine had just gotten back to Chicago, and Tiffany doesn't answer.

Something cracks inside of me as I slide down on the kitchen floor against my cabinets, desperate for anyone who will listen.

As my body begins shaking, Jafar strides into the kitchen, meowing and rubbing his face against my chin. I can't decide if he's trying to comfort me, or just decided it's time for breakfast.

I hold him close anyway, not caring if he tries to bite me or scratch me. I just need someone—or something. Jafar doesn't do either of those things. He just rests in my lap and lets me pet him while the tears stream down my face.

My phone vibrates, and I pick it up, hoping that Milo got my messages.

It's a useless notification about some spam email I received from a clothing company I shopped at one time. I toss my phone onto the carpet of the living room just outside of the kitchen, drowning in my emotion.

I don't even know what to think. Everyone is missing, and I just need someone who cares and understands—someone to listen.

The guilt weighs heavily on my shoulders as I force myself to my feet. I pick up my phone and look through my contacts, hoping to find someone—anyone who would be up this late and be willing to talk.

My eyes catch on Gabriel's number. I never actually deleted it from my phone. I quickly press the call button, knowing that if anyone is going to understand how I'm feeling, it's him.

When Milo and I saw him at the restaurant, he was nothing but kind. In fact, he has always been kind and respectful, so I'm not worried about him thinking that I want anything out of this. He's struggled too, so at least I know he will get this sorrow that is overflowing inside of me.

"Hello?"

"Hey," I say through tears.

"Um, Olive?" he says, his voice sounding unsure. "Are you okay?"

"I—" *I don't know what I'm doing. I'm alone. I need to talk to somebody.* "My grandfather just passed." My voice is unsteady. "I know this is weird, but everyone is asleep. I'm hundreds of miles away from my family, and I just need someone to talk to."

"What about your—" he hesitates. "You're still dating that guy, right?"

"I am." I wipe my nose with my sleeve. "He's great. He just works, and he's probably sleeping. I just need someone to understand." My body starts shaking again, and I know that I'm achieving the best ugly cry of the century, but I can hardly muster up the strength to care.

"Yeah—yeah," he says. It sounds like he is getting up and shuffling around. "I'm dating someone now, but if you just need someone to talk to. There's a diner over on Main that is open all night. If you want, we can meet there in forty minutes. I'll just let my girlfriend know what's going on. She may show up, since this is a little weird."

I think about Milo and realize I should probably let him know as well.

"Right," I say, trying to get control of my emotions. I go looking for something to wear and settle for some sweatpants and an oversized sweatshirt from my college. "I'll let Milo know too."

"Great," he says. "And Olive?" There's a pause on the line, and something settles inside of me as I slip on my shoes.

"Yeah?" I say, running the collar of my shirt over my upper lip to wipe away my snot.

"I'm really sorry," he finally says. There is such a genuineness behind the statement that I'm thankful for his willingness to meet me. I can hardly think around the loneliness that is spilling over my body.

There's also a part of me that is glad he found someone. Gabriel really deserves it.

"Thanks," I squeak out.

"I'll see you soon."

The line disconnects, and I quickly pull up Milo's number, typing out a text message. I don't want him to think the worst, I just want him to know that I needed someone to talk to.

It's not his fault that he's busy.

Me: I'm going to the diner on Main to meet with a friend and talk.

Me: I'm just having a hard time and feel alone. You can come if you want. I'd rather be talking to you.

Sliding my phone in the pocket of my sweatpants and grabbing my keys, I pet Jafar once before heading out the door.

The air is cold, and I'm thankful when my car starts up. I can see a full moon hanging overhead, obscured by the incoming clouds. The clock on my dash reads three in the morning, and I switch the car into reverse and back out of the spot.

On the way to the diner, I can't help but keep my hand on my phone in my pocket. I'm waiting for a response from Milo or Tiffany. Even Corrine or my mother.

Part of me knows that those messages won't come.

As I pull into a parking spot in front of the diner, I look into the glowing lights of the restaurant. The gentle glow almost brings more sorrow to the surface, and I pull down my mirror to check my face.

It's obvious I've been crying, and usually, I would be embarrassed to walk into a public place looking like this, but I don't have the energy to care anymore.

When I walk up to the door, I can see through the glass windows to a booth where Gabriel is sitting, a steaming cup in his hand. He looks disheveled and dressed in a similar sweatshirt and sweatpants ensemble that I'm wearing.

Taking a deep breath, I walk up to the booth.

"Hey," I say. My voice sounds about as small as I feel.

"Hey, Olive," he says, gesturing to the seat across from himself. "Mia said it was fine if I met you. She's actually on her way. I think you'll like her."

"Mia is—" I trail off.

"My girlfriend." There's a satisfied smile on his face, but it's small, as if he isn't willing to show too much with what I'm currently feeling. I'm thankful for that.

"Right." I slide into the booth. "I texted Milo, but he didn't respond. He may still come, though." I let out a forced chuckle. "Then it'll be like a double date."

"We should plan one of those sometime," Gabriel says. "Did you want a coffee? It's my treat."

"That would be nice. Thank you." I wipe my sleeve on my cheek, smearing away the tear that managed to escape.

A pained look overtakes Gabriel's face. "Your grandfather died?"

"Yes," I say, my breath shaking. "I know it sounds stupid, but I was having a hard time over the holidays with it. Something about not being there when my family needs me—about being here and having a good time—"

"It makes you feel guilty," he finishes.

"Yeah." I let out a sigh, thankful that someone is listening.

Gabriel runs a hand through his dark hair. It's darker than Milo's, and my heart squeezes as I wish it was Milo sitting across from me instead.

"Well," he begins, "I'm here to talk, so whatever you're feeling, you can let it out."

With that invitation, and the arrival of a steaming cup of coffee, I unload every last emotion onto the almost stranger in front of me.

TWENTY-NINE

Gabriel laughs at my joke while I sip at my near empty coffee. The tears have subsided, and the pain had numbed into a dull ache.

"Hey, Mia said she's going to be here soon," he says. "I'd love for you to stick around and meet her."

I lean back and blow out a breath. "I should probably head back," I remark. "It's nearly five in the morning, still dark, and I haven't slept. I'm going to end up missing the start of classes."

"That's fine," Gabriel smiles. His hand touches mine on the table. "I'm really glad you called me, Olive." The gesture warms something in me. "If you need anything, just let me know. I hope we can work out a double date."

I smile. "I'd like that."

The door slamming at the front of the diner startles me, and I pull my hand away.

Milo is standing there wearing gray sweats, a thick coat, and tennis shoes. He has a beanie on his head, and the hollowed circles under his eyes tell me he was exhausted.

I try to smile, but it falls when I notice his face twist. There's anger there—hurt maybe, and I look back at Gabriel, my stomach feeling like lead.

"You should probably go talk to him," Gabriel nearly whispers. "He—uh—he probably misunderstood."

I get up from the table, looking over my shoulder briefly. "Thank you for the coffee, Gabriel."

"No problem."

Running out into the parking lot, I nearly slip on the ice. Snow is starting to fall in fat flakes, and dawn hasn't yet begun. The streetlights illuminate the ground, glittering over the leftover snow from the last fall.

Milo is walking fast, desperate to get away. I can see the tension in his shoulders through his coat, and fear pulses through my veins.

He's going to listen to me. I tell myself. *It's just a misunderstanding.*

"Milo, would you stop!" I yell.

He turns around, barely containing the anger and sadness as he walks toward me. He turns away and adds distance before facing me.

"What were you doing with *him?*" he practically growls.

I huff a breath, thick fog floating in front of my face. "Milo, it isn't like that."

"Like hell it isn't!"

Something hard coats my heart, closing me off from whatever this version of Milo is. *He's going to listen.*

"It's not like that!" I shriek, throwing my hands up in frustration. "I just needed to talk to someone. I had *nobody!* Gabriel answered, and we just talked."

A blonde woman walks past us with her brows raised before scuttling into the diner and leaving us alone.

"I was *alone*." I emphasize. "And needed to *talk*."

"And you couldn't have talked to me?" Milo's face twists and I can see the hurt beneath the anger—the thoughts he must be having.

"You weren't there!" I defend. "You weren't there when I needed someone, Milo. That's okay. I know you're busy. I—"

He cuts me off. "You could have waited." His voice is lower now. "I'm here now."

My chest cracks, spilling out the fear of loss that's rising within me. "I couldn't just *wait*, Milo."

His features twist again, and he runs a hand over his hat. "I know that. I—" He's fighting for words. "This is why I haven't dated since college," he confesses. Milo shakes his head. "Olive," he sounds exasperated.

Frustration stirs in my stomach, making me angry. *Why won't he just listen?* I almost want to walk away.

"Olive," his voice is softer, and I look up to meet his brown eyes filled with hurt. "I just—I love you, Olive."

Milo steps forward, crowding my space. Every ounce of anger leaves me, replaced by the welling of tears in my eyes. Time nearly stops at his declaration.

"I have loved you," he continues. "I've loved you since the moment I realized you named your cat after a literal villain. I love the way you blush when I say anything remotely sexual." I can see his breath in the cold night air. "I love the way you sing terribly and most certainly off-key at concerts. I love every ounce of anxiety and overthinking that exists in that body of yours." Milo lets out a breath, his hand moving to cup my face. "I love you."

Pain slices through me when his hand drops away and he steps back.

It doesn't take long for me to formulate my response. Deep down, I think I've known. I've known since the moment he held me at Thanksgiving, or maybe since he was lying on my floor next to me, talking about my fear of the very thing I'm walking through now.

"I love you too," I whisper.

"Yeah, well." His tone hardens, and my legs are shaking from the cold. "That's not what it feels like." Milo's voice raises as he holds out his hand. I can see the anger that he is now feeling. "Do you have any idea what seeing you in there did to me? Do you have any concept of what that felt like?" He's shouting now, and I feel so small. I want to shrink down into the earth.

Looking back, it was a stupid choice—one that made sense in the heat of the moment. One that made sense as I was sobbing on my kitchen floor. But now? I can see how it wasn't the wisest decision to call Gabriel. I should have waited.

Even so, I hadn't done anything wrong. He invited his girlfriend, for Christ's sake.

"It's not like I was cheating on you, Milo." I can hear my voice rising in volume in response. "We were just talking!" The tears finally let loose, and I'm caught between anger, sadness, and desperation. "My grandfather just *died*," I croak out, the sobbing from earlier returning.

"I get that it's hard, Olive." There is no compassion in his eyes, and that part shatters me the most. "But you met with a guy that you *dated*. Do you not see how shitty that is?"

My brows furrow, and I blink back the remaining tears. My teeth should be chattering from the cold, but my face is flushed with emotion, and I can't get a grip on my thoughts. I also can't wrap my head around how difficult this is. It doesn't feel like he's listening to me at all. It also doesn't feel like he trusts me.

"I—"

"Don't even answer that," he cuts me off, taking a step back. "Maybe you don't even see it." He blinks, and I swear I see his own tears being held back while he talks. Despite that, he is still so hardened and harsh in his words. Milo shakes his head as if he's given up. "You're just an immature child," he spits out.

That statement sends me over the edge. I take a step toward him—now desperate. "Milo."

I reach for him, my fingers connecting with the fabric of his coat, but he just shrugs me off. "Don't talk to me," he grinds out.

"Milo, wait." I'm chasing after him now, trying to reach for him—grab his arm. There's nothing I want more than to have him turn around. I'm not above apologies. Maybe what I did wasn't the right way, and I'm willing to own up to that, but this isn't *fair*.

Milo is shutting me out. He opens his car door and I tug on the metal trying to prevent him from leaving.

"Enough, Olive!" He shouts, ripping the door from my grip.

The way he yells at me has my entire body halting with surprise. This isn't the man that I know. I understand what I did was wrong, but this is so far beyond what I expected.

I expected him to listen—to comfort.

I don't know what to say. My mouth hangs open, and I clutch my arms to my stomach to brace myself against the cold.

"I need time to think."

Milo gets in the car, slamming the door, and then speeding off.

I'm standing in the cold with the snow now falling exponentially faster than before. The ice on the ground feels like it's pulling me under, winding up my limbs and covering my skin. The cold has me shutting down.

There really is no other way to describe how I feel now.

Alone.

I glance back at the diner and see the blonde woman who had come in during our fight. She's sitting across from Gabriel and laughing at something he said.

Mia.

Memories with Milo play on repeat through my head, trying to drag me away from the anger and pain he just threw at me.

My phone buzzes in my pocket, and I see my mom's number pop up. The lighting is changing as the sun thinks of coming up. I have class in a few hours, but I'm certain I won't be able to bring myself to go. College is important to me, as are my grades, but somehow, with the world falling apart around me, the idea of sitting through a lecture has me wanting to vomit the contents of my stomach onto the street.

"Hello?" I answer, hearing my mom on the line.

I don't dare tell her what happened with Milo. Maybe it's because I'm ashamed of my own choices. Maybe it's because I think he has a point. It just feels so insignificant despite it all. How selfish would it be to bring up my relationship problems while my grandfather hasn't even been dead for six hours?

I tuck a strand of hair behind my ear, walking solemnly to my yellow car.

"Hey honey, how are you?" she says.

When she asks, I realize how I was never really alone. My mom was just dealing with what she needed to deal with before checking on me.

Immature child.

The insult stings, but I'm starting to believe it as I talk to my mom and get in the car.

Pulling away from the diner, I head back to my apartment, hoping that Jafar doesn't decide to be a complete asshole.

"Everyone is as okay as they can be," my mom confesses.

Great.

Guilt is a heavy thing. People walk around desperate to be right—to be heard. Faced with having their actions or beliefs challenged, they usually behave unfavorably. That's when the guilt sets in. Some people get angry—they scream and holler and defend themselves, hoping to turn it all around and being *right* again.

But I only feel sorrow. I'm falling through a darkened abyss, realizing that the stars Milo talked about, the bright points that allow me to experience sadness and joy in equal measure—those have gone dark too.

"I love you, Mom," I say, turning my car onto the road.

"I love you too, honey."

THIRTY

I took an entire week off of class, barely able to get myself out of bed. My mom booked my flight for the funeral next week, but for now, I'm still stuck on my couch, staring at the fan as it spins around overhead.

Glancing at the floor, I decide to switch positions until I'm stretched out in the same spot. I was in the night Milo was here with me—we were staring at the fan together.

A knock sounds at the door, and I turn to see Tiffany letting herself in.

"It was a really dumb thing you did, Olive."

She isn't one to mince words. I cringe inwardly as she halts in my kitchen, staring at me in the living room in the same clothes as yesterday.

"What are you doing?" she asks.

I close my eyes, fighting all the emotions I don't want to feel. "I'm just trying to disappear," I say.

It sounds so pitiful and dramatic that I'm almost embarrassed, but when Tiffany comes forward and lifts me to my feet, I somehow realize this isn't the end.

There's concern plastered to her face. It's in the way her eyes look over me, as if she's checking me for real physical wounds. "He hasn't called?"

"No." There's a hardness to my tone. Milo hasn't responded to my texts or answered my calls—making him completely absent while I walk through something difficult.

It makes me angry to know he isn't here for me. He just—ran.

Tiffany brings a hand up to brush my hair back gently. "Olive, you need to get out of this apartment. You can't stay here forever. I know that you're upset, but life has to go on."

I groan, throwing myself back on the couch. Jafar hops up and curls himself into a ball on my lap, purring when I scratch him behind the ears. He's been less of an asshole lately, and I firmly believe he knows how awful life has been.

"I know," I sigh, leaning my elbow on the arm of the couch to prop my head up

"Do you want to go out and do something? We can start slow, no concerts. Maybe we could go grab some food to get your mind off of things. We could talk."

"That might be good." Deep down, I know that she's right and sitting inside this apartment for the rest of my life isn't practical. I still can't wrap my mind around the losses. I somehow lost my grandfather and my boyfriend in the same night.

Tiffany comes forward and places her hand gently on my knee, offering a wane smile. "I don't mean to be rude, Olive, but I also think you should consider taking a shower."

Setting Jafar on the ground, I drag myself from the cushions and move toward the bathroom down the hallway of my apartment. "Fine," I say—defeated. "I'm going to take a shower, and then you and I can go out to lunch. Does that sound alright with you, *mother?*"

"Yes, dear!" Tiffany's tone is mocking, and I know she's just trying to look out for me. She's actually here for me—standing in my apartment, and that's more than I can say for Milo.

I glance at my phone before stripping down to scrub my body of sadness. There are no new notifications. I scroll through the text messages I've sent Milo in the past week. The last one was from two days ago. Maybe he realizes I've given up, and he's secretly rejoicing at that fact.

Sighing, I turn on the water and peel my shirt off my body. I get a cleansing towelette and wipe my face, noticing the remains of mascara I tried to force myself to wear yesterday. The makeup did little to help my mood.

When the water is warm, I step into the shower and work to become somewhat of a human being again.

I get out, dry my hair, and put on a pair of jeans and an oversized sweater. My makeup is minimal, and I pull a winter hat on my head to hide the fact that I didn't have the energy to do my hair.

Tiffany is waiting on my floor and playing with Jafar and one of his toys. He scuttles across the ground, trying to capture the pink and purple feathers attached to the stick Tiffany is waving around.

I offer a small smile before speaking.

"Ready," I say.

Tiffany hops up, grabbing my hand and dragging me out the apartment door.

Before I leave, I turn back to Jafar. "Be good. Don't die."

The door closes behind us, and Tiffany already has her car pulled up to the curb when we get outside, as if she expected me to agree to this.

There's still an ache in my chest as we pull away and travel to a local café, but it's easing slightly in the presence of a friend.

At the restaurant, we order all the unhealthy food. It's the most I've eaten all week.

Tiffany and I are laughing in a matter of moments, and the mood lightens considerably.

That's when I feel my phone vibrate on the wooden surface of the table.

We both look down, staring at the device like it has three heads.

"It's probably just my mom," I supply.

"Right." Tiffany seems skeptical, and both of us just have a feeling that it isn't my mother. I've been waiting around for Milo to respond, and even though I'm dreading the conversation that is to come, I miss him, and I'm tired of feeling like shit.

Turning my phone over, I see his name show up on the notification, and my heart starts beating rapidly in my chest.

My hand is shaking as I unlock the screen and click my messages to read what he sent.

Milo: I'm ready to talk, Olive.

I don't know how to respond to him. All I'm doing is staring at my phone when I hear Tiffany snapping with her fingers in front of my face.

"Earth to Olive. Was it him?"

"Yeah." I swallow, trying to decide what I'm going to say to him. I'm caught somewhere between spilling my guts via text message out of the fear that he won't listen to everything else and refusing to respond until he shows more initiative.

I settle for something in between.

Me: When?

It doesn't take him long to respond. Tiffany is staring at me as if I've grown a second head. I'm sure she is wondering what he said, and how I'm going to respond, but I can't bring myself to stop looking down.

Milo: You could come to my place tonight. I work until eight.
Me: That would be fine.

Me: I'll be there.

"What is it?"

I look up at Tiffany and flip my phone, showing her the pitiful messages that decorate the screen.

A smile crosses her face. "Well, that's promising." Her eyes are too lighted to make sense of the messages I received, and when I spin my phone back around, I see exactly why.

There's another message.

Milo: I just want you to know before you get here that I love you. I haven't stopped for a minute.

Milo: And I'm sorry.

Milo: I'll see you tonight.

THIRTY-ONE

The bitter air whips around my body as I stand on Milo's porch. Dim lights shine from the window, but I can't see beyond the empty living room. Night descended swiftly, covering the world in a blanket of blackness that was only broken by the flickering porchlight overhead.

My body is shaking, caught between the cold and the nerves coursing through my veins. I raise my hand to knock, but I can't bring myself to connect to the door. I consider turning back, afraid of what Milo is going to say.

My hand hangs in the air as the door swings open, revealing a disheveled man wearing a fitted black t-shirt, and gray sweatpants. His brown hair is mussed as if he had been running his hands through it with the same nervous energy that I cannot get to leave my own body.

Lowering my hand, and I'm suddenly aware of the snowflakes falling just beyond the porch. My winter hat is damp with their residue.

Milo's eyes have dark circles embedded beneath them. I'm sure I look just as bad considering how the week has gone.

"Come in," he says, clearing his throat before stepping aside to usher me into the house.

I unwind the yellow scarf from around my neck, peel off my hat, and unbutton the gray peacoat I'm wearing. Milo takes it, draping it over the back of his couch.

The gesture is familiar and brings pain to the surface. The room feels suffocating, as if all the air was sucked out—floating away on the wind with all the words left unsaid.

I don't know how to feel in Milo's presence. There is a part of me that wants to apologize for going to that diner and meeting with Gabriel, but there is also a part of me that is enraged by his abandonment.

Regardless of what happened with our relationship, my family still suffered a death. I've had to walk through the loss all week, and Milo wasn't there. He didn't respond to texts or calls. He ignored me when I needed him most. I am not sure how I feel about that, or what it says about the future of our relationship.

If we even have a relationship.

I can't help but question, though, if that is how things will be. When life gets hard and when things get heavy, is Milo going to run. Will he busy himself with work and disappear for days at a time to escape the things he doesn't want to address? Can I even forgive him for doing that to me now? He broke trust when he drove out of that parking lot, but then again, I broke his trust, too.

After talking about it with Tiffany, I realized how awful it must have looked and felt to see me not only confiding in a man at a diner but also a man I had *dated*.

Milo had commented on how Gabriel still wanted to be with me when we were at that restaurant, and even though I knew it wasn't true, not since he had started dating someone else, I could see how the entire situation was destined for failure.

"Would you like some water?" Milo has his hands in his pockets, and my gaze flicks back to the kitchen at the back of the house. I can see Jafar's water and food bowl that he hasn't put away. The image feels like a knife twisting in my chest.

I swallow. "No, no. I'm—I'm okay." I don't really think I am.

Milo nods, barely able to meet my eyes. Something about this room, the scent of vanilla, the heat from the crackling fireplace, it is all working together to make the moment feel more painful.

"I—" I don't know what to say. "I should apologize," I begin, no direction in sight.

"Olive." His voice cracks, and the pained look in his eyes makes me pause. "No," he whispers, shaking his head. I watch as the light from the fire flickers over his face.

As I stare at the man that so thoroughly broke me, I can see the longing behind his brown gaze. Clearing my throat, I look away, unable to bear the weight of it all. It would be nice if things could go back to normal and we didn't have to deal with the fallout of our argument, but life isn't like that. It's messy and horrid, and difficult.

Milo steps forward, and I barely have time to take a breath before his lips are on mine. I stiffen at first, but something in the way he's gripping my face like it's a lifeline has me melting into the familiarity of him.

The tears flow as he kisses me, and I can feel his gentle touch wiping them away from my cheeks. My heart cracks painfully in my chest at the tender touch.

Milo pulls away, pressing his forehead to mine.

"You weren't there," I admit. "The entire time, you weren't there."

Any numbness I was feeling has disappeared in favor of deep sorrow and betrayal.

Milo continues to hold me there, his head pressed against mine. When he speaks, I can hear his pain in the strain of his voice. "I know, Olive. I am so, so sorry."

My shoulders shake as I cry, unable to contain the emotion any longer. "I'm not completely innocent," I say.

"No." Milo's statement halts me. "Do not steal my apology."

I let out a chuckle through the tears.

"Olive, I cannot forgive myself for what I've done to you," he admits. "I forced you to walk through this all alone all week. And guess what? That is exactly what you accused me of in that parking lot. You told me I wasn't there."

I wipe my nose with the collar of my band t-shirt.

"The longer I waited, the more I wasn't there, and the more your words became true. I started thinking that maybe you were right, and maybe you would be better off with someone who could be there for you—someone like Gabriel." He's looking down at me now, face serious. "Then I ran into him with his girlfriend, Mia, yesterday. I felt like the biggest, most horrendous asshole ever. When he told me he hadn't talked to you since that night, I—"

"It's okay," I whisper.

"It's not." Milo brushes another kiss on my lips. "I will spend the rest of my life regretting what I did to you. I wanted to call you every second of every day."

I let out a soft laugh. "My cousin Jo told me she loves when men grovel in books. It's her favorite thing."

"Well, I'm not trying to get Jo to take me back. How do you feel about groveling, Olive Finch?"

I lift one shoulder casually. "It might be nice," I admit.

"Then I'm going to grovel." Milo shakes his head before kissing me again. "I will grovel forever if that would make you forgive me."

Milo runs his thumb over my cheek.

"God, this is so cheesy," I admit.

"It has to be," he says. "You're the main character right now. It absolutely has to be cheesy."

I wrap my arms around him, dragging him closer and burying my face in his chest. His scent wraps around me, and I finally release all the tension I've felt for the past week.

Milo strokes my hair in a gesture so gentle it nearly breaks me. It reminds me of Thanksgiving, and when I stood in the hall as he comforted me.

He may have really messed this up, but he is capable of being there. He has been in the past.

"I love you," I whisper into his chest.

"I love you, too."

EPILOGUE

A year and a half later.

Milo's sister, Jamie, is sitting next to me while I play one of my favorite Curly Fries songs. She's been really interested in music lately, but honestly, I think she is interested in anything I'm interested in.

I'm just glad she likes me.

His parents were easy to get along with. They were both extremely kind and respectful during our trip to Colorado last summer, but Wilfred and Marie really love hiking. I like hiking too, but when they said a short hike, I really thought they meant *short*.

Not an eight-mile hike.

My legs still hurt just thinking about it. Milo finished his residency, and since Dr. McMillian was retiring, he was more than happy to take his place.

I moved out of my apartment toward the beginning of last summer, and I haven't regretted it for a single day.

"Okay, but the real question is, why *Curly Fries?*" Jamie seems disgusted with the name of the band, and I snort because she absolutely has a point.

"Maybe you can send in a request for them to change it," I remark. "Though I hardly think that will work."

"Maybe when you and Milo take me to a concert, maybe the drum player will fall in love with me, and then I'll be able to choose their new name." Jamie looks up at me with a smirk on her face, and I am fairly certain she believes the drum player will, in fact, see her and fall in love with her.

Honestly, it wouldn't be surprising considering she takes after her brother in the looks department.

I deadpan. "Jamie, I highly doubt that."

Jamie swats my arm and stands up, making her way to the sliding back door of Milo's house.

Correction. Our house.

"You're no fun, Olive. Don't you even believe in love?"

"Of course she does." Milo sits down on the bench next to me, winding his arm around my shoulders and kissing me on the temple. "She just doesn't believe in love at first sight. When I first asked her out, she seemed completely preoccupied with deciding how many radishes to purchase, and slightly annoyed."

I laugh, remembering the radishes from the supermarket.

Milo's mother, Marie, sits down across from us with a fruit bowl she places on the patio table. I pick up a piece of watermelon and pop it in my mouth, thankful for the heat of summer. It won't last long, though. Winters in Minnesota are brutal.

Wilfred sits down next to his wife, and I smile at the way his gaze flicks over her face. If Milo's parents are anything, they are in love.

And incredibly athletic. That damn hike was brutal!

"I'm going to go in and check the rolls." Milo says, turning and getting off the bench. He goes through the back door into the house, and Wilfred and Marie are smiling at me without saying a word.

"So," I say, uncomfortable. "Where's Jamie?"

As if she heard me, Jamie walks out of the house, holding her maxi dress up off the patio.

"I think Milo needs help with the rolls," she says. "He may be a fantastic doctor, but he can hardly cook water. Too bad you're a poor cook too, Olive. You both are going to starve for the rest of your lives."

I point a finger at her. "One, there are plenty of restaurants in our area, Jamie. And two, we can always invite your beautiful mother and she can cook for us."

Wilfred tips his head back and laughs, his voice booming out. "Right," he says. "No offense, honey, but you can't cook either."

Marie scowls at him, and I chuckle as I make my way to the sliding back door to find Milo.

When I enter the kitchen, he's nowhere to be found, and the oven is off, rolls discarded on the stove. The pan is still warm.

I walk back to the bathroom, but Milo isn't in there either. The bedroom door is cracked, and I press my hand against it gently, seeing him stand next to the bed with his back to me. The door creaks when I nudge it open.

Milo moves quickly, shoving something in his pocket. Something inside me wakes up, making my heart pound in my chest.

"What are you doing?" I ask.

"Thinking," he says. His hands are both in his pockets when he turns around with a wide smile on his face. I can't help but be suspicious. I'm not an idiot.

It is suspicious.

"I swear to every god in the universe, Milo. If you dare pull out a ring in front of your parents or anyone, I will say no before you can even finish your sentence."

The smile never leaves his face as he steps forward. Milo drags me toward him, pressing his lips to mine. "You're a fun ruiner. Did you know that?"

"And you're bad at grammar."

"My goodness, Olive Finch. Did you really come in here just to be mean to me while I stand before you with a ring in my pocket?"

"And you—" My heart nearly stops. His face hasn't changed, and I can tell he's pleased with himself. He's caught me off guard, and he definitely thinks he has won. The sad thing is, he has. "What?" My voice is barely audible.

"I'm not going to get on my knee," he says. "You told me two months ago that it would be *embarrassing*." He uses air quotes around the last word, and I snort.

"That's beside the point," he continues, shoving his hand back in his pocket.

I can barely breathe as he pulls out a small box, opening it to reveal a golden band twisted to look like vines with a round green emerald stationed in the center. I look at the ring, and back at Milo—absolutely speechless.

"Did you plan this?" I say.

"No, not really," he confesses. "Well, I did. I was going to do it at a concert. The stage, flashing lights, the works."

I cringe inwardly.

"What made you change your mind?" I ask.

"Eh," he starts. "Jamie said that it would thoroughly embarrass you, and I figured I shouldn't do that. Getting your menstrual cup stuck in your vaginal canal was probably enough embarrassment for the rest of your life."

"This is going really well."

"Oh good. I'm glad you like it." Milo holds the ring up higher. "So—" he says, awaiting my response.

I smile up at him, barely looking at the ring he's still holding between us.

"I guess I could get behind marrying you. You *are* a doctor."

Milo laughs, and it's probably my favorite sound. There's something so genuine about the way he expresses joy. "What does that have to do with anything?" he asks.

I waggle my eyebrows. "You know, marrying for money. I always told Elias that I'd be a rich aunt."

"You're ridiculous."

Milo pulls the ring out of the black box and carefully slides it on my finger.

It isn't long before I hear the door to our bedroom creak open. His parents and Jamie are standing there waiting expectantly with smiles on their faces. Marie is holding a phone, and I can see my family in the picture of her FaceTime call.

I glance back at Milo before Jamie walks forward, practically shouting.

"What the hell did she say?"

I hold up my hand, and I can hear the collective awes float into the room. My cheeks flame, and I'm ready for the ground to swallow me up.

"Oh, this is terrible," I groan.

Milo sighs, wrapping his arm around my shoulders. "Maybe," he says. "But at least it's terrible with me."

The End

Acknowledgments

I truly have so many wonderful people to thank when it comes to the making of this novel. I always feel so strange writing these acknowledgments, but I feel that this particular one is important.

I want to start by thanking my editor and dear friend, Kenna. You seriously have no idea how much I love and adore you. For every single time, you have called me within thirty seconds of me texting you a writing question, for the time I randomly decided to write a Romantic Comedy and you squeezed it into your schedule, I cannot thank you enough for your talents, but more importantly, for who you are.

I have to thank my cousin, Olivia, for providing most of the hilarious material in this book. I'm so glad that your life is playing out like a romantic comedy, and someday you will truly find a Milo Jameson. I hope you enjoyed seeing the pieces of your life woven with whatever crazy ideas I came up with. I love you so much. Thank you for being more like a sister than a cousin (also insert me cursing you out for moving to Minneapolis because wtf was that?).

I want to thank my family. I hope you enjoy reading this story as much as I enjoyed writing it because it truly is filled with so many pieces of us.

Ali, you are such a bright spot in my life, and I'm so thankful for all the ways you gas me up about my writing. You're a fantastic narrator and a more fantastic friend.

Finally, my husband, you're the reason I decided to pursue writing at all. I couldn't ask for a better partner in this life. You've spent over ten years getting to know me, and for some reason, you still like hanging out with me. Thank you for supporting me, being my closest friend, and being such a fantastic father to our son. I love you.

Also, thank you, dear reader, for supporting me in this author's journey. I could literally do none of this without you.

TIGGER WARNINGS

239

Discussions of Depression
Closed Door Sexual Content
Mentions of the Death of a Pet
Death of a Grandparent
Brief Discussions of a Mental Health Facility

The Misadventures of Olive Finch Playlist

Half of Your Love by Bahamas

Buttercup by Hippo Campus

South by Hippo Campus

It's Called: Freefall by Rainbow Kitten Surprise

All That and More (Sailboat) by Rainbow Kitten Surprise

Cool God by Jack Symes

Caroline by Briston Maroney

BUICK by Raffaella

Minnesota by Samia

Hush Hush by The Band CAMINO

Keep Driving by Harry Styles

Daylight by Harry Styles

honey by Coastal Club

All Too Well (10 Minute Version) (Taylor's Version) by Taylor Swift

Kilby Girl by The Backseat Lovers

You Are In Love by Taylor Swift

If Only by Hanson

Death By A Thousand Cuts by Taylor Swift

New Year's Day by Taylor Swift

Marigolds by Early Eyes

Next to You by John Vincent III

About the Author

Emmie J. Holland is the pen name used by Emma Steinbrecher for her romance books. Emma Steinbrecher typically writes New Adult Fantasy and New Adult Romantic Comedy.

She lives in Ohio with her two dogs, her son, and her husband.

When she is not writing, she enjoys hiking, learning new hobbies, and reading.

If you're anxious to read any of her other works, here is a list of the books.

<u>A Clan of Wolves Duology</u>

A Clan of Wolves by Emma Steinbrecher (Book 1)
A House of Witches by Emma Steinbrecher (Book 2)

<u>The Death Hunting Trilogy</u>

The Death Hunting by Emma Steinbrecher (Book 1)
The Raidan Awakening by Emma Steinbrecher (Book 2) Releases October 2022
Title and Release Date To Be Announced (Book 3)